The Cleanup MAN

ENGINEERED BY THE LORD
AUTHORED BY G.S.CREWS

Debo

Thank y_
your Exper_
I Hope you
enjoy the
Read!

_eorge

You Are
Wonderful!
I love your
3Pirit!

Crews Publications Presents, The Cleanup Man

This novel is a work of fiction. Any resemblance to real people, dead or living, actual events, organizations, establishments, and/or locales are intended to give the fiction a sense of reality and authenticity. Names, characters, places and incidents are either products of the author's imagination or are used fictitiously, as are those fictionalized events and incidents that may involve real persons and did not occur or are set in the future.

The Cleanup Man Copyright © 2007 by G.S. Crews

Published by:

Crews Publications

PO Box 1698

Jonesboro, GA 30237-1698

Phone: 770-617-9688

Email: crewspublications@yahoo.com

Edited by: Asta Editorial Services

Library of Congress Catalog Card No: In publication data
IBSN-10: 0-9795236-1-3
IBSN-13: 978-0-9795236-1-8

Dedication

THIS BOOK IS DEDICATED TO
ELLEN G. CREWS: MY MOTHER,
MY BEST FRIEND, AND MY INSPIRATION.
YOU WILL NEVER EVER EVER BE
FORGOTTEN.

Chapter 1
The Breakup

At the corner of Peachtree Street and 4th Avenue in the vibrant city of Atlanta, Georgia, a fire red coupe pulled up to the red light. At the same time, a couple and their son walked out of the front glass doors of a condominium after enjoying their Thanksgiving day with a family friend. They looked both ways. As they crossed the street to their parked Chevy Yukon, their teenage son recognized the flashy car that sat at the red light.

"Mom, that's a Bentley GT. It's worth three hundred thousand dollars!" he exclaimed.

"That's not worth, baby. That's foolishness."

The mother coolly unlocked their SUV using the remote control located on her key ring. The family stepped inside the vehicle. A breeze slightly ruffled the hem of the mother's tan slacks.

"I saw the rapper T.I driving a car like that in one of his videos, mom."

The teenager imitated the rapper by twisting and dipping his shoulders from right to left.

"That's what's wrong with you young kids now! Watching BET and DVD, and not R.E.A.D.I.N.G.!"

The seatbelt light dimmed as everyone secured themselves in their seats. After checking her blind spots, the mother pulled out onto Peachtree. The discussion about reading continued.

"Reading is power," she declared.

"Mom, I read, just not all the time!"

"Reading the manual for your new video game doesn't count, son. Do you know why I read the magazines about investing?"

"Why?"

"'Cause they make me aware of how to use other people's money to make more money!"

"That's right, baby. People are making more money than ever by making investments work for them," the teenager's father informed.

"Well, I'm going to own my own game design company," the teenager informed. "Are we going to the King Center and put some quarters in the fountain?"

"Yes, we are. We are going to go show thanks to the man who made it possible for us to be free!" the father said.

As they drove down the street, the teenager stared at the chrome rims of the vehicles as they sparkled in the warm evening light. The black rubber of the passing cars hugged the grimy asphalt.

"One day, I am going to roll like that," the teenager vowed to himself.

The teenager looked back and saw the Bentley's tag with the abbreviation of 1LFE2GV. At that moment, a flock of pigeons flew nearby and let loose a shower of bird poop that splattered on the Bentley's windshield and hood.

Splat! Splat!

The driver's door of the fire red Bentley opened up and a young woman dressed in tight jeans and a camisole leapt out of the car and shook her fists in the air.

"You stankin' birds!"

The drivers behind her shouted when the light changed to green. "Get out the road, you crazy broad!"

However, the lady didn't hear the disgruntled drivers. Her eyes were fixed on the flock of birds as they flew past a nearby billboard that caught her attention. She read the sign aloud, "Vanity…All is vanity." The woman shook her head, hopped back into her vehicle, and sped away. The pigeons continued to fly. They veered in and out of the buildings until they came to a parking deck that was conjoined to a state of the art condo that rested in the middle of Atlanta.

On the twenty-fifth floor of this condo, an attractive lady sat Indian-style on the edge of her sleigh bed. She checked the time. It was 4:30 in the afternoon. All was not well for this young lady. Her name was Tomeka Williams. She was dressed in a pink v-neck blouse and designer jeans. Her long brown hair swooped along her shoulders and specks of glitter shimmered along her neck. Although, she was dressed to impress, Tomeka was very upset with her boyfriend as they engaged in an intense argument over the phone.

"Antone, I made Thanksgiving dinner for us and you stood me up! Why are you acting like you're ten years old?" Tomeka yelled.

Tomeka brushed her long brown hair out of her face as she patiently waited for Antone to give her an excuse for not coming to her house for Thanksgiving. The silence grew as Tomeka stared at the clock on her wall. The second hand completed a full revolution before Antone made a sound. However, it was not the sound that Tomeka wanted to hear.

"Huh?"

The sound triggered Tomeka's more aggressive side.

"What are we doing here, Antone? Am I not woman enough for you or is it that you're not man enough for me?"

The last question cornered Antone between responsibility and foolishness. Antone rubbed his low-cut wavy hair. He had nowhere to run. He knew it was time to address the situation.

"Tomeka, I have constantly told you that I am not ready for a relationship."

This mundane excuse transformed Tomeka's aggression to fury.

"Stop it, Antone! News flash—men and women who sleep together are in a relationship!"

Antone did not reply. This was not the first time a woman had informed him that it was time for him to grow up. His child's mother had tried that constructive criticism approach when it was time to sign his son up for tee-ball. It had backfired and caused her bipolar disorder to become unstable. However, this time he actually cared about the end result of the situation.

"What are you suggesting?" Antone inquired.

"It's time for us to move forward."

Antone bit his bottom lip. He knew that if he crossed the line of total commitment, then there was no going back. He gathered himself. The decision was made.

"Tomeka, I am not ready for a relationship," Antone replied sternly as he slid off his jeans and put on a pair of sweatpants.

The unexpected response choked Tomeka. Angry tears formed in her almond-shaped eyes.

"AKK!"

"Tomeka, are you okay?"—Antone became worried when he heard only silence—"Tomeka!"

Tomeka cleared her throat. Her fury was now at high-tide.

"You were ready to sleep with me last night and the night before!" Tomeka screamed as tears streamed down her face.

Antone pinched the bridge of his nose as he listened to Tomeka cry.

"Tomeka, please calm down!"

Tomeka did not stop crying.

"Y-you are always ready to dim the lights and p-play some love songs but you are not ready for a relationship," Tomeka sobbed.

"Tomeka, I never meant for it to be like this."

"For two years! I-I've given you two years of my life!" Tomeka cried.

"Tomeka—"

"Y-you are a punk!"

"Tomeka—"

"Y-you're right. You are not ready. You are sorry."

Tomeka's sobbing subsided as she regained her composure. Antone moved the phone away from his ear and looked into the speaker. He listened as Tomeka's irate voice shred his character.

"I tried! I tried, but what can a woman do when her man wants to act like a boy?" she lamented.

Antone put the phone down for a brief moment. It was time to end this once and for all.

"Tomeka, I—"

"You are just like those raggedy sheets on your bed—used and worn out!"

Antone became angry. Tomeka knew that he was sensitive about residing at his mother's house. Not everyone was financially stable like she was. Having a baby by a star football player had its perks.

"Tomeka, you need to calm down. I am not going to tell you again?"

Tomeka's eyes grew wide! *Has this Negro lost his mind?*

"What! Who do you think you are talking to?"

"Tomeka, you're acting like a spoiled brat."

"How dare you!"

"This is no dare, Tomeka! It's over! You hear me! It's over!"

Those last harshly spoken words doused water on Tomeka's fire. She collapsed on a body-sized pillow. Her auburn hair swept across her face. Although she was devastated, she was not defeated.

"Antone, I will scream at any man who leads me on a wild goose chase for two years!" Tomeka retaliated.

"You—"

"You should get a life!"

Tomeka closed her flip phone. The call was over. She was single. Antone was completely out of her life.

Antone tossed his phone on the bed. He remembered when they went to the store and purchased their matching phones.

"Good-bye and good riddance."

Antone stood up from his bed and took off his light blue button-down shirt. In front of the mirror that was attached to his dresser, he flexed his chocolate six-pack abs and broad chest.

"Back to the basics, my boy," Antone said to his reflection.

He put on a white tank top and exited his room. As he stepped into the narrow hallway, Antone's environment enveloped him. He stood in the dingy hallway and studied the walls that needed to be painted. However, what stood out more than the walls was his twice-divorced brother, Mike. He wore an over-stretched brown tank top and a pair of green cargo shorts as he lounged on the brown couch watching *The Pirates of the Caribbean*. Used cups and glasses were scattered across the coffee table in front of him.

"First, you get married. Then, you fuss," Mike joked. "Then, you find yourself lying on a couch with a heavily starched wardrobe because she took you to the cleaners!"

Antone studied his brother as Mike propped his crusty feet on a stack of pillows.

"You should patent that ghetto footrest you just invented and sell it at Shop-Mart," Antone said.

"Yeah! Yeah!" Mike waved Antone off as he turned the volume up to the movie. Mike used to be a stylish, distinguished, man-of-the-hour kind of brother. Back-to-back divorces could leave a person on the couch literally.

"My life is like a movie," Antone said as he started back down the hallway.

As he neared the bathroom, he heard the loud expulsion of air. Antone soon smelt a sickening odor.

FLAH! FLAH!

"Ugh! Gabriel, you stank! Use some spray, turn on the fan, or light a match," Antone yelled as he ran to the other bathroom located in an adjacent room.

Antone closed the door and looked in the mirror. It was time for a self-check. His brother was lying on the couch like a shipwreck and his nephew was stinking up the hallway.

"Antone, you traded the Atlanta skyline, a romantic dinner for two, Marvin Gaye quietly playing on the stereo, and scented candles bordering a garden bathtub for this! Now, you can't even use a bathroom that smells decent! You're messing up!"

The blaring sound of rap music snapped Antone from his contemplation. Antone stormed out of the other bathroom and back to the bathroom door he had passed earlier. Not only was the music too loud but the shower was running at full blast.

"Turn that music down!" Antone yelled as he banged against the door.

The music continued to blare. Antone banged against the door again.

BANG! BANG!

"Gabriel, turn down the radio!"

From behind the bathroom door, a deep voice yelled back.

"Go use the other bathroom! I'm shaving!"

"Are you shaving in the shower?"

"No!"

"Well, why are you wasting water? Everyone in this house is crazy!"

Antone stormed to his room and slammed the door. He walked over to a picture of his mother that sat on his dresser. Since Antone's mother had passed from breast cancer, his family seemed to be on a downward spiral with no sign of redirection.

"Mom, where are you?" Antone asked.

He glanced at the digital clock. Only thirty minutes had passed since the argument and he was already missing Tomeka.

"I remember when life was simple. Boy meets girl. Boy and girl go to mall and take pictures. Boy buys girl birthday gift, they both buy Christmas gifts, and the cycle repeats. Then, girl wants boy to eat Thanksgiving dinner. Boy knows this is the first step to loosing freedom, so boy breaks up with no hard feelings."

An empty feeling had formed in Antone's stomach. It was similar to the panic one feels when he can't find his debit card after withdrawing money from an ATM. It was a troublesome feeling.

"Boy makes bad decision. Boy is stupid."

Antone glanced at his wall where there was a collage of R&B posters. The poster of the extraordinary female group, Xscape, caught his attention.

"Who can I run to…?" Antone quietly sang to himself.

Antone laid on his bed until he fell asleep. Tomorrow was Black Friday, the busiest shopping day of the year. You could get everything from 32-inch flat screen televisions for four hundred dollars to DVDs for five dollars. For one day, civilization slipped into madness as shoppers searched for the best deals. For Antone, it was an exhilarating feeling. Sine he was the photo lab manager at Shop-Mart, he had to be ready to greet the high volume of holiday shoppers with a coupon and a smile.

As Antone slept, Tomeka called the representative for their cell phone provider. She terminated the services and made sure that the final bill would be sent to Antone's address.

"No more ties that bind," Tomeka said.

She strutted to the balcony and gazed at the city. The shadows of the nearby skyscrapers loomed over the smaller buildings. Tomeka glanced to her right. In the distance, she saw the red lights of the CNN building. Not faraway, the lights of Centennial Park twinkled. She watched the tiny groups of people converge as Atlanta's exciting nightlife took shape. She took a deep breath. It was the perfect evening to take a ride downtown.

Antone, I wish I could see your face when you try to use your phone, she thought. She closed the glass door to her balcony and picked up the keys to her Lexus truck. While preparing to leave, her cell phone rang. Tomeka glanced down at the caller ID screen. The caller was none other than her best friend, Peyton.

"What's up?"

"What's up? Umm…are you okay?"

Peyton quickly detected the sour mood her friend was in. She was a country white girl with wonderful intuition. She took pride in knowing what was on a person's mind.

"Just because we played volleyball together in college, you think you know when I am having a bad day," Tomeka replied.

"Tomeka, I know you like a fisherman knows how to fish!"

They laughed. Peyton always amused Tomeka with her country sayings. When the laughter died down, Tomeka confided in Peyton.

"Me…Me and Antone broke up."

"About time you and that sapsucka split. We are going to the club this Thanksgiving weekend to celebrate! Whooooweeee!"

Tomeka was not startled by Peyton's reply. Peyton was from the other side of the tracks and had a "tell it how it is" attitude. However, Tomeka knew when to let Peyton know she had overstepped her boundaries.

"Peyton, you're acting like *you* just broke up with your man!"

Peyton quickly apologized.

"Oh, I am sorry. How do you feel?"

"Terrible. I feel like I lost a part of me. You know?"

Peyton pulled her shoulder-length blonde hair into a ponytail.

"Lost like a celebrity's morals or like a little kid's puppy?" asked Petyon.

Tomeka giggled. Although Peyton was five foot seven with sea blue eyes, she was as smart as a genius and as down to earth as a bum on the street. She knew exactly how to make Tomeka laugh.

"Lost like you just woke up with my fist in your eye?"

They giggled more. The sound was crisp and refreshing. Peyton continued to evaluate her friend.

"Tomeka, let's look at it from this vantage point. Antone stays at his momma's house and works at Shop-Mart!"

"And?"

"Oh, for loving grace and Christ's sake! He is the manager of the photo lab! A machine could do his job! You can't build a future based on security like that!"

Tomeka cocked her head to the side. Only Peyton could blast Antone and get away with it.

"I know you are not talking about security! With your job as a flight attendant for Coffee, Tea, or Me Airlines, the only security your man knows is the one that calls the police if someone breaks into your house!"

"My man takes care of all my needs," she said slyly.

As they talked, Peyton flipped through a brochure of New Orleans and the French Quarter. Tomeka switched the conversation back to the focal point.

"I broke up with Antone because he told me he wasn't ready for a commitment."

"Tomeka, didn't your mother tell you that blessings come in disguise?"

That comment annoyed Tomeka. She became quiet. Peyton thought that the call had dropped.

"Hello? Tomeka?"

"I'm here. Enough about me and my problems. What are you doing?"

"I was just getting some things together for my three-day trip to

New Orleans. I leave on Sunday, so that means we have to go out tomorrow night."

Tomeka had a flashback and said, "New Orleans...Byron Smith... Ummm mmm!"

Peyton rolled her eyes.

"There you go thinking about your baby daddy, the highest paid football player in the league!"

"He is cool to a certain extent. Unfortunately, that extent goes as far as the next lady. That dude would hump a tree if he couldn't get splinters!"

The two women giggled at the thought.

"At least your baby daddy was a freak. Jack was slugger. He beat the snot out of me," Peyton confessed.

The admission silenced the laughter. Tomeka had seen pictures of Peyton's swollen eyes, bruised arms, and bloodied lips. Jack was a low-life serving five to ten for assault and battery. He had beat Peyton while she was pregnant.

"I'm sorry, Petyon. I didn't mean to make you think of your baby daddy."

"It's okay. He just creeps me out."

"To be honest, Byron gives me the creeps, too," Tomeka admitted. "That is why I never take Janicia to visit him. When he cheated on me, he hurt me deep."

"A person who cheats has no conscience."

"I'm thankful that he provides this lavish lifestyle for Janicia and me, but I still keep my guard up. Last week, he mailed me a card asking if we could get back together."

"Do you think you will?"

"I can't say. Byron has to show me that he has changed for the better."

"Well, you are better than me, girl! I would have been in the Superdome cheering the New Orleans Pirates to victory every game from the get-go! My ole man is as lazy as a bean in a burrito!"

"You are going to run that man off," Tomeka said.

"Girl, I wish I could trade him in for a scooter or something!"

Peyton sat at her bar and poured herself a glass of scotch-on-the-rocks. Her flight attendant hands moved without spilling a drop on the countertop. Juan Suarez, her husband, sat in the living room with their daughter. They were watching a Thanksgiving Day football game when a commercial for the newly released DVD, *The Pirates of the Caribbean,* flashed on the screen.

"Here he comes!" Juan shouted.

The star running back for the New Orleans Pirates rushed across the field as a rioting gang of zombie pirates chased him. The speedy running back was Byron Smith, Tomeka's baby's daddy.

"Is that the commercial?" Tomeka asked.

"Yeah, that's my man," Peyton replied.

Suddenly, Tomeka's phone beeped. She had an incoming call on the other end. It was her other best friend.

"Peyton, Shelby is beeping in. Put me down for this Friday at Caribbean Nights. I'll brief Shelby."

"You know Shelby has to do those stupid international workout shows on Thursdays and Fridays!"

"She doesn't have one scheduled tomorrow. Her husband is closing a big deal in Miami today and her mom is baby-sitting for her tomorrow. It will be like old times!"

"While you do that, I am going to go tell Mr. Suarez to scoot over on the couch so Mrs. Suarez and Itty Bitty can watch a movie. Too much football will damage your brain," Peyton joked.

"Okay. Tell Itty Bitty I said hello and tell Mr. Suarez that the New Orleans Pirates are gonna stomp all over the Atlanta Tigers!"

They ended the call and Tomeka clicked over, but there was dead silence. Her friend had hung up. Tomeka quickly accessed her contacts and clicked on the name Shelby Harrington.

Shelby was dressed in black tights and a blue spandex vest. She was putting away the remains of the Thanksgiving dinner that she had not had a chance to enjoy when her cordless phone rang.

Beeeep! Beeeep!

She barely heard the phone ring because of the loud noise coming from the nearby theater room where her twins, Sidney Gabrielle and Alexander Ryan, were watching the *Pirates of the Caribbean*. She rushed over to the stand and picked up the phone.

"Hello?"

On the other end, she heard the explosive sound of laughter.

"Are you all at the movies?" Tomeka managed to ask through her laughter.

"Um…no. It's the twins watching a video. Hold on."

Shelby covered the phone's mouthpiece with her hand and screamed at the top of her lungs.

"Sidney Gabrielle! Alexander Ryan! Turn the volume down! Mommy is on the phone and is about to record! Thank you!"

The volume did not get lowered. Tomeka continued to laugh.

"You are confusing those kids by using two names as their first names! They are going to be wearing plaids and stripes!"

"You used to wear army boots with swimsuits and that didn't affect you," Shelby laughed.

The two women laughed aloud. The laughter healed a little of

Tomeka's aching heart. Tomeka was glad to see that Shelby retained
her down-to-earth personality while living in her elaborate $1.2
million dollar home in Dunwoody. Tomeka always knew she could
confide in Shelby.

"I have something to tell you. Do you have time?" Tomeka
asked.

"Yes, Hon, I have a little time. I have a satellite workout session
that starts in the gym in a couple of minutes."

Shelby always called Tomeka Hon, short for Honey. Shelby's
husband had been coined Mr. Fitness and had several satellite classes
that Shelby taught. In about five minutes, a small portion of the
southern tip of France would be following her instructions.

"Antone couldn't commit, so he had to quit," Tomeka said.

"Ah! I kind of liked him. I thought he was your yang."

"My yang?"

Shelby slipped on a pair of gray cross-training sneakers as she
explained the concept to Tomeka.

"Your yang is your equal opposite. He kept you balanced. Do
you remember that preppy guy you met in college?"

"Yeah, I remember Zachary and his polka dotted bow ties!"

"Well, you both were yin. He didn't balance you. Do you
remember what you did to him?"

Tomeka smiled as the memory returned to her.

"I made him a fried bologna sandwich with a cold glass of sugar
water!"

They both exploded in laughter. As the laughter died down,
Shelby finalized her explanation.

"See with Antone, he would have seen through the misdirection.
He would have eaten the sandwich but spilled the water!"

"You're right. All Zachary wanted was to be seen with a black girl because he thought it made him look blacker, but Antone should have made a way to stay with me."

"At least you don't have to deal with his baby's mother anymore."

Tomeka let out a sigh of relief.

"You know one day she told me that she was going to take me out like the trash."

Shelby laughed.

"You should always count your blessings," she reminded Tomeka.

Shelby walked into her mirrored studio gym. There were three tread mills, two elliptical machines, four benches, and a combination machine with a lateral bar. There was already a high-end camera set up with a closed circuit monitor on a stage. All Shelby had to do was turn on the switch and she would be ready to broadcast.

"What was Peyton talking about? I never hear from her since she became a flight attendant," Shelby said.

"Same as usual. Oh yeah, she wants us to go to Caribbean Nights tomorrow before she goes to New Orleans."

"Put me down on the list. I could do for a little night life and a double shot of tequila," Shelby said.

As Shelby stretched in front of the mirror, she thought, *Who has ever heard of working on Thanksgiving?!* Even though she hated to admit it, her husband was a little off balance.

"Well, I know you have to put on your show. Call me tomorrow," Tomeka said.

"Alright, Hon. Talk to you soon," Shelby said.

She ended the phone call and turned the phone off to keep it from interfering with the recording of the session. Shelby walked to the stage and flipped the switch. The camera came on, but there was a message on the monitor that read 'No Signal'.

"This has never happened before," Shelby said.

She checked all of the connections. Everything was as it should be.

"I guess I will be taking the kids to mom's house earlier than scheduled," Shelby said as she turned off the camera.

Shelby walked out of the gym not knowing that it would be her last time inside that room.

Tomeka zipped up her brown suede jacket as she stepped out of her door. She caught the elevator down to the parking garage where she hopped into her Lexus truck. She pulled out of the parking deck. As she took her evening drive, Tomeka conferred with her party girl alter-ego, Lady T.

"Tomeka, what's wrong?"

"Antone's gone," Tomeka answered.

"We did have some good times."

"Several but you can't keep living like that," Tomeka replied.

"You're right. It's for the better. I'm going to miss his sexy smile, though," Lady T said.

"It's for the better."

"Tomorrow is your night," Lady T said.

Tomeka cruised down Peachtree Road toward Atlantic Station. She was at peace with her decision to dump Antone. Tomeka pressed play on her compact disc player and Tina Marie's angelic voice resonated through her speakers as she told a story about a Portuguese lover. The lovely tune took Tomeka's mind back to a time when love was everything and not just anything.

At 9:30 p.m., Antone was startled out of his sleep by a knock at his door.

BANG! BANG!

"Quit beating the door and come in!" he yelled.

The door opened and in stepped his towering six-four nephew. Antone sat up on his bed. His tired eyes squinted against the light. He spoke first.

"Dang, Mustafa!"

"Telephone, punk."

Gabriel threw the cordless telephone at his uncle. Antone barely caught the cordless before it smashed into his face.

"You're lucky that I'm fast."

"Yeah, you lucky! Ha! Ha!"

Gabriel continued to laugh as he closed the door. Antone looked down at the phone. The number on the caller ID was for his child's mother, Mary.

"Why didn't you call my cell phone?"

"Poor Antone, You don't even know that your phone has been turned off!"

"Off?"

Mary laughed uncontrollably.

"Yes. Off. Disconnected for non-payment!"

Antone could not believe the news he had just receiving.

"This can't be happening," Antone said.

"Antone, I told you that rich girl didn't love you! You are a duck!"

Adding more insult to his injury, Mary continued to laugh. Goosebumps formed on Antone's arms. He hung up the phone and fell backward on the bed. Somehow, someway, he had to get back into the game.

Chapter 2
The Soap Opera

4:50a.m

A crooked line of shoppers stretched from the entrance of the Shop-Mart and around the building. Black Friday had come and so had the ladies and gentlemen looking for the perfect gift at the lowest price. Standing at the entrance of the Shop-Mart was a group of security guards who were committed to keeping the peace. The chief security guard was an older white man dressed in a tight gray uniform. His belly poked out like the infamous Boss Hog from *Dukes of Hazzard.* He strode forward to make an announcement in his southern antebellum accent.

"Ya'll listen up, hea. Ten minutes 'till the store opens."

"Discounts! Discounts!" the crowd chanted.

The chief security guard nodded his head. Not too faraway from him stood a fair-skinned mother with a short stylish haircut and her two daughters. They had been standing in line for an hour and a half just to have the privilege of being one of the first to enter the store.

"Mom, Latreese is going to love that CD player that you can attach to the bottom of the cabinet," said one of the daughters.

"Yes, she is. She spends so much time in the kitchen cooking our dinner."

"Yeah, now, she is going to be dancing and cooking. I hope she can do two things at one time," said the other daughter.

The women laughed. At that moment, the security guard stepped forward.

"Y'all listen up, hea. Tis less than five minutes! I need you to take three big ole steps back!"

The mother and the daughters took two steps back. On the third step, the mother accidentally stepped on someone's foot behind her. Immediately, she wheeled around. Standing before her was a medium height overweight dark-skinned black lady dressed in a black tee shirt and baggy jeans. The mother noticed the dark areas along the woman's cheeks, her visible facial hair, and the two short braids tipped with pink bows.

"I'm so sorry."

The large lady replied in a husky voice, "You better be."

The mother, although smaller, was not daunted.

"Huh. The nerve!"

Another large woman poked her head from around the large lady's wide shoulders.

"I ain't neva scared! I ain't neva scared!"

The two women began bouncing, holding each other by their shoulders, and chanting the phrase over and over.

"Ignorance is bliss," the mother said as she turned around.

Suddenly, the large woman shoved the mother in the back. The mom fell on her knees.

"Mom!"

The two daughters rushed to their mother's aid, helping her to her feet. As she slowly rose to her feet, the mother spoke to her daughters.

"That's it! Marla. Carla. I am your mother; but, right now, I am about to stomp a mud hole in this woman's butt! Yah!"

The mother wheeled around and kicked the large woman in the stomach.

"Humph!"

The large woman leaned forward, holding her stomach.
Then, she fell to her knees. The mother spit in the palm of her right
hand and slapped the woman across her face.

Wham!

The other woman ran to her friend's aid and wrestled with the
mother as her daughters kicked the first large woman on the ground.

"Whoa! You want some of the Ruby Smack Down, too!"

The security guards rushed to break up the fight. Right when
they left their posts to stop the fight, the rowdy crowd rushed into
Shop-Mart.

5:30 a.m.

Crowds of shoppers inundated the aisles of Shop-Mart for the
super savings. Antone worked the photo lab with his co-worker and
friend, Walt. Walt wore a pair of khakis with a matching Shop-Mart
blue polo shirt, while Antone wore a blue button-down with black
slacks. They watched as an angry woman pushed her filled cart past
the photo lab and knocked a stack of folded shirts over.

"Antone, they are tearing up the store! You had better do
something since you are the 'HNIC' in this camp," Walt said.

Antone ignored his friend's comment. Antone knew that showing
the slightest interest would feed into Walt's exaggerated persona.
However, Walt continued.

"Did you see that six-woman brawl earlier? Somebody opened a can of whoop—"

"Watch your mouth!" Antone interrupted as he smiled through clenched teeth.

Another woman, pushing an over-stuffed cart, eavesdropped on them. At that moment, a cordless phone fell off the top of her pile; it sent a cold shiver down Antone's spine. The memory of Mary's phone call was still fresh in his mind.

"Ow!" Walt yelled.

Antone wheeled around to see Walt moonwalk across the floor and load the printer.

"This isn't a dance audition. Please do your work and quit playing around!"

Walt slid over to Antone, placed his hand on Antone's forehead, and, in an Irish accent, said, "Tone, yer stayed up to the wee hours of d'night. Tossin' an' turnnin' like a babee. Yer thoughts were plexed from the wierding."

"Walt, quit it!"

Antone walked away from Walt.

"Don't youse walk away from me," Walt said as he mocked the dialect of a black slave.

Antone giggled. That giggle was all Walt needed to put on a comedy show.

"Yo! Son! I am from New York, son," Walt said as he imitated a youth from New York. "You know we go back like car seats and braids!"

Antone smiled as another customer walked up to drop off pictures to be developed.

"When can I pick up these pictures?" the woman asked.

"Yo, son! I got mad fat skills on this printer, son!"

"Ma'am, you can pick up your film as early as Sunday if you wish. Thank you for shopping at Shop-Mart of Tara Boulevard," Antone said in a professional manner.

"Is he special?" the woman asked as she pointed at Walt.

Antone nodded his head.

Once the customer was out of sight, Antone pulled Walt to the side and scolded him.

"Didn't you see I had a customer, Walt?

"Yo, son, the world turns!"

"I have an image to uphold here. I am the photo lab manager!"

"Got a little steam under your shirt, huh, trooper! No late night snacks from the Mrs., huh?"

The statement pushed Antone's button.

"Quit asking me about Tomeka! We don't date anymore!"

"Well, that is a good thing."

"Why do you say that?"

"Because you won't feel guilty about what is coming our way. Put your game face on 'cause I'm about to deal the cards! Deuces are wild," Walt said as he regained his composure.

Antone turned his head to see two fair-skinned ladies approaching them with a handful of disposable cameras. The foremost woman was the eye-catcher. She had long black hair. Antone liked how the woman's stylish denim jacket, black skirt, and black tights fit her slender body. Tomeka was fine; but, compared to this vixen, she was out-classed body for body! As the vixen walked toward the counter, a disposable camera dropped from her hand and hit the ground. The camera tumbled behind her two-inch black heels.

"Aw, man! I hope it isn't broken," she wondered aloud as she stooped down and picked the camera up.

Her friend, who was dressed in a pair of dark wash jeans with a pineapple v-neck camisole, stooped to assist her. Walt stared at the women's butts.

"I think I just went blind because I don't see a panty line," Walt muttered.

"Stay focused!"

Antone pretended to organize some completed tasks in a nearby cabinet. Walt licked his fingers and smoothed out his bushy eyebrows and mustache as the women neared the photo lab. Walt rushed out to greet them.

"How come, I…I mean, how can I assist you lovely fine specimens?" Walt asked.

He stretched out his right hand to shake the friend's hand. She walked past Walt without any acknowledgement.

"Good morning, ladies," Antone greeted them as he flashed a smile.

"Ooohh, girl, he has dimples! Look at that smile! It's picture perfect," the attractive lady exclaimed to her friend.

Her friend, however, was not impressed.

"Calm down, Sameka! You are overreacting!"

Antone glanced at Walt. The read was seamless and invisible to the naked eye. Walt leaned on the counter and addressed the intervening friend.

"What's happening, shawty? A woman like you needs a man like me. I have more hardware than Home Depot," Walt boasted.

"Whatever?"

"Me and you, your cousin and her momma, too, could be rolling in my Daewoo to Checkers for a burger tonight," Walt continued.

"You have me mistaken."

Walt leaned forward and frowned.

"I didn't want to holla at you anyway. Your breath smells like the back of an elephant's—"

The friend drew back her hand to slap Walt, but Antone caught it just in time.

"Be easy," Antone said as he released her hand.

"That bastard better watch his mouth! I want him fired!" the friend yelled.

"I will deal with him. Walt, go to my office! I will see you there in a minute," Antone yelled.

"But—"

"But nothing! Go! This is your last day! I've had it with you!"

The friend rolled her eyes at Walt. The three of them watched as he walked toward the layaway section. When Walt disappeared, Antone turned his attention back to the ladies.

"I am sorry. He is bipolar. His parents can't afford the medication. I try to diversify my employees, but this is just unacceptable," Antone said.

Antone placed his hand on his forehead and shook his head.

"Is he crying?" the friend asked.

"I think so," Sameka answered.

The ladies watched Antone fight back tears. Sameka was moved by his sensitive side.

"I-it's okay...um, I didn't catch your name," Sameka said.

"Antone. And you are?"

"Sameka."

"I assure you this will never happen again. As a courtesy, Mrs.

Sameka, I will develop your pictures for free and you can pick them up on Monday."

"Thanks, but I am not a 'Mrs.'. I haven't met the right man."

"Perhaps your luck just changed," Antone said as he pointed to his last name on his nametag which read Wright.

Sameka laughed. She adored a man who had a sense of humor, charm, and sensitivity. Antone seemed to possess those characteristics plus a degree of professionalism. Where she was from, guys like Antone did not exist. She could not let this opportunity pass her.

"I want you to come to Caribbean Nights tonight and have a drink with me in the VIP. My friends are throwing me a birthday party. Here is my card. Will I see you then?"

"Breezy."

Sameka quickly autographed the back of the card with her signature and handed it to Antone.

"Show this card to whoever is at the front door so you can get to me."

Antone nodded his head as he placed the card in his shirt pocket. Tomeka continued to fade away. Sameka and her friend walked away. Antone stared at how her hips moved as she walked.

"God bless the one who made you," Antone said.

Just as they were about to round the corner, Sameka looked over her right shoulder and gave Antone a wink. Antone winked back. Just like that he was back in the game.

5:45 a.m.

Shortly after Sameka and her friend left, Walt returned to the Photo Lab. He gave Antone five and they tapped each other's fists for a job well done.

"Say, cousin, did you get the number?" Walt asked.

"Man, I got the business card like a pimp," Antone replied in a high-pitched voice while patting the left pocket of his shirt.

"My man."

"I am going to be sippin' on something blue or brown with Sameka Edwards tonight in the VIP at Caribbean Nights! Holla at ya boy!"

"Tone, you are the biggest P.I.M.P I have ever seen. We have an image to uphold. Let's get some work done!"

Antone and Walt continued their work in the Photo Lab. Things for Antone were beginning to turn around.

7:00 a.m.

The alarm clock rang and startled Tomeka from her sleep.

"Ahhhhhhh!" Tomeka screamed as she kicked the covers from her.

She looked wildly around her bedroom. Earlier that evening, she had indulged in a frozen Margarita with extra shots of Patron. She was waking from a nightmare where she had competed in a celebrity death match. She could not distinguish the person's face but Tomeka sure did know that the celebrity had gotten the best of her.

"What did the bartender put in that drink last night?" Tomeka moaned.

She rolled out of the bed in her red camisole and briefs. Tomeka slipped on her purple cashmere robe with matching slippers. Then, she turned on the television that was mounted on the wall.

"Today is going to be a gorgeous Black Friday; however, the weekend will take a turn for the worst as a severe cold front approaches," meteorologist Fred Michaels predicted in his navy double-breasted suit.

He pointed at the animated word 'frigid' as it crept from north to south on the television screen.

"Enjoy this last day of sunny skies. Today's high will be in the 70s and the low will be in the 60s tonight. Tomorrow will be very different. April, back to you."

"The percentage of lonely single women has dramatically increased since last year according to a website survey," April the anchorwoman reported.

"Sister, I am living proof," Tomeka said as she poured herself a mocha latte.

Tomeka flipped open her phone and searched for Peyton's name. She fired off a text message to Peyton with hopes that she would want to go to the mall with her.

"If anyone can advise me on finding a man, it will be Peyton. I can't go another two days like this."

Tomeka sipped her morning beverage and waited for her friend to respond. Little did Tomeka know that her next two days would be filled with life-changing events.

9:00 a.m.

Shelby opened the door to a Victorian-style home located in the suburb known as Jonesboro. She walked into the home with her two kids and sent them into the adjacent bedrooms. Shelby was dressed in a pink sport thermal top with black Capri pants. This was not only her birth home; it was also the place where she got her hair done by her older sister, Latreese. Shelby inhaled. The smell of bacon was amazing.

"I am here for my nine o'clock appointment," Shelby announced as she closed the door.

At the sound of the announcement, two of her four sisters exited their mother's kitchen to greet the unexpected visitor.

"Appointment?" Latreese exclaimed.

Latreese, Shelby's oldest sister, was the most talented of her sisters. She was the cook, the hair stylist, and the lawyer. Latreese wiped her floured hands on an old pair of drawstring jeans. She had just finished making biscuits.

"Yep, my hair appointment," Shelby answered as she hugged her sister.

"You were supposed to be bringing the twins, not getting your hair done! Where are they?"

"Waking up your children in the other room," Charlene answered as she stood with her arms crossed.

Pancake batter was on the sleeves of her brown shirt. She also wore jeans with an embroidered floral design.

"I see you two are cooking breakfast. Do you need any help?" Shelby asked.

"Yeah, you can do the eggs," Charlene answered.

"Seems as if your stomach is in bacon grease withdrawal," Latreese said.

"No, the bacon is calling me," Shelby replied as she held her stomach.

Being married to a fitness guru had its perks as well as its pits. Bacon and other red meat were public enemy number one at the Harrington's residence.

"Come on and help us, so I can do you hair," Latreese replied.

They retreated into the kitchen.

"Where is Benjamin?" Charlene asked.

"He is opening a new gym on the east coast," Shelby replied as she removed the carton of eggs from the refrigerator.

"When is he gonna quit putting his business before his wife?" Latreese asked.

The question was touchy. Shelby became defensive.

"He is doing what is best for his family."

Charlene and Latreese exchanged knowing looks.

"We are concerned because we are your family," Charlene said.

"Yeah, concerned like when Marla told you all that Benjamin was gonna leave me for a young girl," Shelby said as she greased the skillet with butter.

"Let's just drop it and cook," Latreese said.

For a moment, they cooked in silence, and then Shelby spoke.

"Where are Marla and Carla?"

"They are shopping for bargains with mom at Shop-Mart. I hope they don't get in any fights with those crazy customers," Charlene said. "Mrs. Ellen asked about you, Shelby."

At the mention of Mrs. Ellen's name, Shelby felt bizarre. Mrs. Ellen had welcomed them into the neighborhood after prostate cancer took their father's life. Mrs. Ellen quickly became a part of their lives. She was like a grandmother to them.

"Really?" Shelby exclaimed as she put the fried eggs in a dish. "How is she?"

"She is the same healthy old lady. Mrs. Ellen still goes fishing on sunny days and she still visits the sick and shut-in. That lady is a godsend!"

"I will try to catch her at home before I leave this afternoon," Shelby promised.

After the three women finished preparing the breakfast, they called the children to eat. Shelby missed being with her family. Lately, Benjamin's schedule had been overwhelming. Hopefully, things would slow down after the holidays.

10:00 a.m.

Northbound traffic on Georgia 400 had been a breeze for Tomeka, but she knew it would change when she ventured onto the surface streets near the mall. She had zipped full speed on the interstate while listening to her Missy Elliot CD. Pulling up to Peyton's house, she parked alongside Peyton's silver Infinity Q45 and 2003 black Maxima. Tomeka hopped out of her Lexus truck. She was dressed in a three-quarter sleeve cabana blue crewneck, straight-leg jeans, and a pair of cabana blue stiletto ankle boots.

"This is the last day I am going to be alone," Tomeka said as she closed her car door.

She walked up the winding driveway past the decorative boulders with surrounding shrubbery and stopped at the front door of Peyton's brick two-story home. Tomeka glanced around at the community. A pleasant breeze blew through her hair as she made out the distant shore of a silvery lake bordered by a group of thin green trees.

The next date I go on is going to involve a walk around a lake. Tomeka thought.

She rang the doorbell and soon heard the sound of approaching footsteps.

"Girl, you got here just in time," Peyton said as she opened the door dressed in a lavender tank and a denim skirt with a pair of rainbow striped slides on her feet. Her blond hair hung past her shoulders.

"What's wrong?" Tomeka asked.

After Peyton locked the front door, they walked to Tomeka's car.

"Don't believe the hype about that "Latin Lover" stuff! We may need to stop by the adult store later!"

Tomeka laughed as they hopped into the car.

"I am not going to feed into that nonsense. Juan is a hard working man who loves his wife and baby," Tomeka said.

"Tomeka, I never met a man who was as lazy in bed as Juan," Peyton said.

"Maybe he needs vitamins."

Peyton scoffed.

"This is not about what he needs. It is about what Peyton needs and what Peyton needs is for her boots to be knocked!"

Tomeka maneuvered the vehicle through the community. She knew that Peyton was a complainer by nature and was never satisfied.

"Well, maybe his job is stressing him out. After all, he is the highest paid software engineer at the largest phone company in Atlanta. The pressure to deliver must be overwhelming," Tomeka reasoned.

"Read my lips—it has to go up for it to go down," Peyton said.

Tomeka laughed.

"Look where you came from. You were with a man who beat you and dragged you through the mud. Now, you are living better than good. You are living great!"

"Your point?" Peyton asked.

"You are rocking a Louis Vuitton graffiti pouchette! They only made 5,000 of them. Why are you complaining? You are with someone who worships you!"

"Someone can live with you and you can still be by yourself, Tomeka," Peyton said. Then changing the subject, she asked, "Which mall are we going to?"

"Well, I really wanted to go to Neiman Marcus in Lenox so I could get something for tonight."

"Okay, Lenox it is."

"Peyton?"

"Yeah?"

"Can you help me work on my moves? I've been out of the game for two years," Tomeka said.

"Say no more! I can help you get what you want!"

"I don't want to catch any germs!"

"Think positive. Tonight is our night!"

Tomeka smiled as she drove toward the mall. *Tonight is going to be unforgettable and tomorrow will be the beginning of new things.*

10:45 a.m.

Shelby leaned back in her chair at the dinner table and loosened the button of her Capri pants.

"That was a good meal, Charlene," she exclaimed. "You put your foot in the grits and sausage!"

"I appreciate it," Charlene responded. "Even though you have maids who cook all that healthy food for you, you didn't do that bad yourself."

"If Benjamin ever saw me eating a meal like the one I just had, he would have an aneurysm!"

"Shelby, do you still have that cute personal trainer?" Latreese asked curiously.

"No, Nathan landed a large contract with a prominent wrestler."

"Too bad. I was hoping to see him again. I remember when I saw him helping you stretch. He was showing all those biceps, triceps, neck muscles, leg muscles...ahhhhh! That man could pick up the world like Atlas!"

"Latreese, I hate to tell you this but he is a member of the Rainbow Team. He has a VIP card to all the gay clubs in Atlanta!"

"Stop lying!"

"You could show up at his door in nothing but your Vicky Secret's and all he would say is, 'That's cute. How much did it cost?'"

The sisters burst out laughing just as the telephone rang.

"It hurts me to my heart to see all that man go to waste! I can't believe that Mandingo brother has gone over to the dark side," Latreese laughed as she answered the cordless telephone in a joyous voice.

"Hello?"

An automated voice answered her.

"You have a collect call from a correctional facility. Do you accept the charges?"

"Huh?"

"You have a collect call from a correctional facility. Do you accept the charges?"

Latreese laughed louder.

"What's so funny?" Shelby asked.

"Someone is calling from a correctional facility."

"You have a collect call from a correctional facility. Do you accept the charges?"

"Hang up the phone, Latreese," Charlene advised.

"I want to hear this poor soul's voice. He may just want someone to tell him Happy Thanksgiving."

Latreese wiped laughter tears from her eyes.

"Yes, I accept."

The automated service connected to the caller. The voice of the caller sent a chilling sensation down Latreese's back. The voice did not belong to a wretched criminal. It belonged to her loving mother, Ruby.

"Latresse! Is that you? What took you so long to answer the phone? I need you to come down to the jail in Lovejoy and bail me, Marla, and Carla out! We sort of got into a scuffle at Shop-Mart! Hurry up! Call Shelby!"

The automated service disconnected the phone call. Latreese stood silently before her sisters with a slack jaw. Waiting for her to move, Charlene and Shelby stared blankly at their older sister. When Latreese finally spoke, her voice was just above a whisper.

"Charlene, I need you to stay here with the kids. Shelby and I have to go bail Mom, Carla, and Marla out of jail. They got in a fight at Shop-Mart."

Shelby and Latreese gathered their things and rushed out of the house. They sped through the neighborhood in Shelby's 745 BMW. They had to get to the bondsman as fast as they could.

11:00 a.m.

Meanwhile, Tomeka and Peyton walked through Lenox Mall with shopping bags in their hands. They neared a group of vendors selling shades and various fragrances. Tomeka stopped at the vendor. After a few minutes of browsing, she purchased a pair of sunglasses. During the purchase, she overheard the conversation of a nearby teenager and another vendor.

"I'm saying how much for that chain?" the teenager asked as his friends crowded around him. He was the only person in the group who did not have one and was tired of looking out of place.

"For you, my friend, fifty dollars," the vendor replied in a heavy Middle Eastern accent.

He modeled the silver chain. The jewelry sparkled in the light.

"Fifty dollars! This chain better not turn my neck green," the young teenager exclaimed.

Tomeka and Peyton strutted past them. At the sight of the two women, the group of men ceased their conversation. All eyes followed the passing ladies.

"That is how women should look and smell," the young teenager said as he sniffed the enticing fragrance of the two women.

"Only in America," the Middle Eastern vendor remarked.

Tomeka and Peyton headed toward Neiman Marcus.

"The mall is packed. I have never been to this mall the day after Thanksgiving," Peyton said.

"Just wait till Christmas," Tomeka advised.

"There are some cute guys in here, too. Look at that one over by the escalator!"

Tomeka turned to her right and saw exactly what her friend saw—a guy in a gray Marthe Girbaud denim jean suit talking and laughing with a cluster of his friends. He had a low fade with deep waves.

His smile makes Antone's look like burnt macaroni and cheese!

For a moment, Tomeka and the guy made eye contact.

What are you doing? You are not over Antone! Don't fall for that smile! DON'T DO IT!

The thought caused her to quickly snap out of the trance.

"Tomeka, are you okay?" Peyton asked.

"Y-yeah."

"You got it bad!"

"Yeah, I guess I am not over Antone," Tomeka admitted.

They entered Neiman Marcus.

"Tomeka, if a person doesn't want to be with you, then you cannot make him."

"I just thought we had something special. One day, I want to be married and have a family. I thought we were headed in that direction."

They stopped to examine a rack of designer jeans.

"Marriage is overrated. I would die to have someone exchange a look with me like you and that guy just did!"

Tomeka raised her eyebrow at Peyton's comment about marriage. For Tomeka, marriage was a sacred vow. It was not a passing fad!

"Peyton, you don't mean that about marriage, do you?" Tomeka asked as she thumbed through a rack of blouses.

"Tomeka, you know I was just kidding," Peyton said as she tossed her a pink shirt. "This would look good on you."

Tomeka held up the shirt. She liked the shirt and could see herself in it. She stretched out her hand and spoke in a proud voice.

"Tonight, the diva returns and I am going to do it for every woman that has been led on a wild goose chase over the waterfall of inconsideration, quicksand of depression, and stagnant swamp of broken promises!"

"Oh, my God! Are you running for president or shopping for a new outfit for the club," Peyton asked while blushing.

An older couple observed Shelby and Peyton intensely.

"I think she is going to steal that shirt," the older woman said.

"She might be on that stuff," the older man commented.

Tomeka apologized to the store's customers.

"Umm, I'm sorry. I guess I got carried away. I just got out of a two-year relationship."

The people shook their heads at Tomeka. Peyton and Tomeka continued the rest of their shopping in silence. Tomeka, however, kept thinking about going to the club with her friends. She couldn't wait for the night to come.

11:30 a.m.

Latreese and Shelby waved from a distance as the glass doors separated in the jail. On the other side, their mother and sisters waved back. Their mother was a slim, light-skinned lady in her late forties. Ruby was still jazzy – keeping fresh on the latest styles and always keeping her eyebrows arched.

The doors opened and two muscular deputies escorted the three women down the walkway. The deputies looked like male strippers to Latreese. She tried to dismiss the thought as her mother cried out, "Latreese! Shelby! My babies! Lord Jesus, thank you!"

"Mom! Carla! Marla," Shelby shouted as they all embraced.

"You all have a good day," one of the deputies said as he returned to his post.

"Thank you," Latreese said.

"You all got here quick! I wasn't expecting you to come for at least a couple more hours! The Lord works in mysterious ways. Amen," Ruby said as she kissed each of her kids on the cheek.

"Yes, He does, momma. I was supposed to have a recording this morning, but I couldn't get a signal so I went ahead and came down early," Shelby said as she tightly hugged her mother.

"Thank you, Jesus," Ruby said.

"Let's get away from this ugly place," Shelby said.

The five women quickly exited the cold shadows of the building and piled into the pearl white 745 BMW.

"Shelby, do you have that song by Sean Paul and Beyonce?" Marla asked.

Carla giggled as she pulled her hair back into a ponytail.

"That's what we should have been singing instead of 'I Ain't Never Scared'," Carla laughed.

"Ya'll were rowdy, huh? What was mom doing?"

"Chanting and bouncing, too," Marla said. "That's what started the fight. I hope that our records aren't messed up for eternity!"

"So, ya'll started the fight!" Latreese said. "Don't worry about that, Marla. I have friends who will chop those charges up and wash them down the drain."

Ruby cleared her throat. It was time for her to cleanup the situation.

"No, we did not start the fight. We were standing in line and the security guard told everyone to step away from the door," Ruby explained. "As we stepped away from the door, I accidentally stepped on this woman's foot. I quickly apologized. Then, someone started yelling that absurd song. You know how your cousins are!"

"Yeah, I know how we can be," Shelby said as she passed up a slow driver in the fast lane.

"Well, everyone started bouncing! Then that big lady—I swear she was bred by whales and giants—pushed me to the ground. She didn't even apologize. That's when your sisters showed off that kung fu fighting they learned from those Jackie Chan movies!"

"It doesn't stop there," Marla continued. "Two other big ladies came to help out their friend! It was a three-on-three grudge match when Momma got up! Momma, kicked that first lady in her knee, spit on her hand, and slapped her against the wall!"

"Mom, you laid the smack down to that lady," Shelby laughed.

"Yes, she did. Mom, you could be a wrestler," Carla joked.

"I am who I am—a bad mother," Ruby said as Shelby pulled into her mother's front yard.

After the car came to a complete stop, the women got out of the car.

"Hey! They're back," Charlene and the kids yelled as they ran outside to greet them.

At the top of the hill, a slim older lady in a white Florida t-shirt and aqua blue pants watched the scene below. She was about to embark on her morning stroll around the block.

"It's getting warm. The fish will be biting soon. First, I need to talk to Shelby. She has to know," the lady said.

Everything was happening just like she had dreamed. Now, the last thing that was left was for Shelby to come see her so that she could tell her what she had seen with her own two eyes.

Noon

City: Atlanta

Temperature: 68

Feels like: 72

Jack, Peyton's baby's father, stared at an online weather report. Tattoos of red fiery devils chasing nude women stretched along both of his arms. His brown stringy hair reeked of sweat and cigarette smoke. His blue work uniform was sordid. Jack had not changed his clothes since he was fired from his job two days earlier. He had slipped into madness.

"They need me. I am Jack Holmes, the best mechanic in Nashville!"

Jack picked up a bottle of beer and turned it up to his mouth. Nothing came out. Jack angrily smashed it on the floor.

"No more devil water but one line of powder for the power."

He took out a rolled up dollar bill and snorted his last line of cocaine.

"Whoa! Owww! Hot damn!"

A burning sensation ripped through his nostrils and right up to his brain. Jack swung a powerful right hand at the computer that sat on his desk. The computer crashed on the floor.

"Now, that is an effective spam blocker!"

Jack walked over the empty potato chip bags, liquor bottles, and beer cans. His black workman boots crunched the trash as he made his way to the bathroom. He stood in the mildewed bathroom and stared into a smudged mirror.

"Soon, it will be over," he assured his reflection.

Jack stared at the bags under his eyes.

"Soon, we will be in the upper room. Me, Peyton, and Itty Bitty."

Jack picked up a torn magazine that featured spearheading software designers called "Software Extraordinaire". While he was locked up, Peyton had sent him a taunting letter detailing how she was going to be in a magazine with her new husband, Juan Suarez. It wasn't long before he asked the prison librarian to subscribe to the magazine. Juan and Peyton, who was nine months pregnant at the time, were on the cover of the fourth issue.

"Juan Suarez and his beautiful wife Peyton Suarez reside in Alpharetta, Georgia, a suburb north of Atlanta. They are expecting their first child," Jack read aloud. Then to himself, he said, "Correction. That's my child."

Jack's prison sentence was supposed to have been five years, but he only served eighteen months. On the first day of his freedom, he had found out through the grapevine that Peyton had relocated to Georgia with his daughter. That day, Jack decided that it was time re-start his visitation rights.

"Sixty-eight but it feels like seventy-two. When I leave Atlanta, it's going to be four-hundred degrees and counting."

He washed his face in cold water and dried it off. He changed into a black sweatsuit and checked the contents of his gym bag.

"Shovel, military knife, black gloves, and infra-red pistols with extra clips. In four hours, you will see the grave that I am going to dig for you, Peyton. I am going to toss you six feet below Georgia alive!"

Jack stormed out of his apartment and hopped into his black '89 TransAm. He sped toward the interstate. In four hours, Peyton was going to have a reality check.

1:00 p.m.

On the other side of town, Antone had just checked out from work. He stood with his hands on his hips as he inhaled.

"The day went by fast and furious," he exclaimed.

Antone entered the pedestrian zone at the same time the driver of a small gray Ford pick-up careened around the corner. With his left knee raised and his forearm over his face, Antone cringed and prepared for impact. The driver slammed on her brakes and skid to a halt. By the will of God, the out-of-control car swerved left and right and halted just inches away from Antone.

"You focking moron! What are you trying to do? Get ran ova or something, jeeze!" the female driver exclaimed in a heavy Bostonian accent.

Antone blankly stared at the rude driver, yet managed to speak.

"I am in the pedestrian crosswalk! I have the right of way!"

The female driver did not reply. She just sat with her head out the window and stared at Antone with a curled lip.

Is that person really mad or is she just scared?

Antone thought it would be nice to find out. Antone frowned. Then, he reached under his Shop-Mart vest. The driver's eyes widened as she jerked her head back into the vehicle.

"Ahhhh! Don't shoot! Let me live!"

Antone quickly withdrew his hand from his vest. His hand held his favorite brown rectangle lens shades. Antone coolly placed the sunglasses on his face and strolled away.

The angry lady peeped out of one eye and watched as the young black man walked toward his white Camry with chrome tires. The white car backed up. When it was totally backed out, the wheels turned in her direction. Slowly, the car moved toward her.

"Oh, no! He's going to do a drive-by!"

The lady fumbled at the car's gears, but it was too late. The white car had pulled alongside her. The tinted driver's window rolled down. Instead of a hand holding a gun, the extended hand held a coupon.

"This coupon is for a free disposable camera. Thank you for shopping at Shop-Mart of Tara Boulevard."

The lady took the coupon with a shaking hand.

"T-thank you," the lady said.

The tinted window rolled up and the white car drove away. The lady looked down at the detailed information on the card. The card did not say anything about a free camera. The card was a business card that read, 'Sameka Edward's Accounting Firm'.

"This ain't no discount card for a free camera!"

The woman ripped the card into tiny pieces and tossed the litter out of the window. The wind caught and then scattered the pieces. Antone was going to have an unpleasant surprise when it was time to use the card.

2:00 p.m.

Tomeka parked her truck in Peyton's driveway.

"So, what time do you want to meet at the club?" Peyton asked as she stepped out of Tomeka's truck.

"I want to do something different tonight," Tomeka replied.

"Something different, like what? You want to enter the club like a superstar, huh?"

"Yep, just like old times! I want all of us to meet at the IHOP and creep down Peachtree in a straight line with our music loud enough to cause an ordinance!"

"Girl, you are trying to do it big, huh?

"Big like an elephant," Tomeka assured.

"Well, I will meet you at IHOP at 10:45. I am going to take a nap. Talk to you soon."

Peyton closed the door. Tomeka waited until she had safely went inside before pulling off. As she turned out of the community, she saw Peyton's hair comb tucked away in the compartment on the passenger's door. Suddenly, her cellular phone rang. Assuming the caller was Peyton, Tomeka answered the cell phone in a sassy tone.

"Yeah, trick! I found your comb in my man's car! When I catch you, you ole blonde-headed bimbo, I am gonna put some fingerprints on you for messing with my man!"

There was a moment of silence over the airwaves.

"Say something! I can hear you breathing!"

"Um, excuse me. I was calling for Lamar."

The smile on Tomeka's face vanished at the sound of the deep masculine voice with a slight southern drawl. Tomeka realized her mistake and apologized.

"Oh! I'm sorry. There is no Lamar at this number. You must have the wrong number."

"I am sorry, Ms. Lady. I hope I didn't disturb you."

"No, you didn't. Have a nice—"

"I don't mean to interrupt you or bother you, but you have the most pleasant voice a lady could have. I know this is strange but I am the owner of the nightclub Caribbean Nights and would like to see you in there tonight."

"Oh, really," Tomeka said.

"Champagne will be falling from the ceiling like rain. I want you to be there to enjoy it. It seems like you need a break from some drama that has occurred in your life."

"Thanks, but I can buy my own drinks."

"What I am offering transcends the concept of free drinks. I am offering you the opportunity to leave your troubles on the dance floor."

Tomeka was speechless. Finally, she put together a series of pronunciations to form a coherent sentence.

"I don't have drama like that. I really thought you were one of my friends, and I was trying to play a joke on her."

"Then, I will see you tonight?"

"I had already made plans to be there anyway."

There was nothing in the caller's voice that made her uneasy. This guy seemed genuine and sincere.

"I am glad you did make plans, but it gets better. First, go to the valet parking area and tell the valet personnel that you are a friend of John Wane."

"Like the duke?"

"Just a different color. The valet will park your car for free. Then, go to the VIP line and say that John Wane sent you. Walk down the corridor and talk to Britney. She will put a florescent green band around your wrist. This will give you unlimited free drinks and access to any of the VIP rooms."

"Is this a joke?"

"No, it isn't. You will be allowed up to two guests. I just want you to have an excellent time in my club. I want this night to be memorable."

"Okay, John Wane. We will see if this is a hoax or something."

"And your name?"

"Ms. Eastwood. Nice to talk to you, John Wane."

"Same here. Enjoy yourself tonight."

The call ended, but she could not get the man's voice out of her head. It was the effort that he had given. He seemed to possess a kindness that had been alien to her for so long. She had almost forgotten how it felt to be appreciated. Hopefully, tonight would be her night.

3:00 p.m.

Inside the home of Juan and Peyton, a stinky smell filled the hallway. Peyton was in the bathroom when the phone began to ring.

"Juan, can you answer the phone? I am in the bathroom! Sheeesh!"

"Got it," Juan yelled as he rushed into the kitchen.

The phone was on its third ring when he answered it.

"Hello?"

There was no response, but Juan heard breathing on the phone.

"Hello? Is anyone there?" Juan inquired again.

He clearly heard the caller's breathing. The city's ambient sounds could be heard in the background, but the caller did not say anything. The caller continued to breath.

"Hello!"

Finally fed up, Juan ended the call. Before he could place the cordless phone on its base, it rang again.

This time, Juan carefully looked at the caller ID display on the phone and mentally memorized the phone number. The phone number had a 504 area code. If this punk tried to give him the silent treatment again, he would report the number to the authorities.

"Hello," Juan answered.

"Sorry, I have the wrong number," the caller said.

Before the caller hung up, Juan distinctly heard the popular song "Slow Jamz" playing in the background. When the call ended, Juan quickly redialed the number he'd stored in his mental memory bank.

"Thank you for calling the Omni Royal of New Orleans. My name is Seynthia. How may I help you?" the front desk clerk answered in her New Orleans southern belle drawl.

"Um, yes, ma'am. I…well, someone just called from this number and hung up."

"I am sorry, sur, but we have beaucoup rooms up hea and we can't monitor every person calling in or out."

"Yes, you are correct. Thank you for your time."

Juan hung up the phone with a bundle of uncertainties enwrapping his mind. The doubt knocked Juan out of balance and gave way to his split personalities—the angel and the diablo. The angel was always peaceful and pleasant. The diablo, however, was aggressive and rude.

That guy was calling for Peyton! The diablo yelled.

No he wasn't. He had the wrong number. The angel soothed.

That was Itty Bitty's dad! Peyton's estranged lunatic ex-husband. The diablo growled.

The angel spoke with assurance. *No, that was just a man with the wrong number.*

Don't fool yourself, Juan! That Peyton is hard to please! She is always complaining! She is fitty fied! The diablo snarled.

She is a great woman who makes you better. Peyton is for you and only you. The angel argued.

The diablo drove home all the facts.

That was another man calling for her from New Orleans and that is where her next flight is to take her! Juan, you can take the woman out of the trailer park but you can't take the trailer park out of the woman.

"Juan, who was on the phone?" Peyton inquired.

"No one really. He had the wrong number," Juan replied.

"It took you long enough to answer it. We should hire a maid to answer the phone because you are too slow."

"I'm sorry. I'll do better next time."

Peyton walked into the kitchen. Juan held his peace. He could not believe that Peyton had another man. He needed something more concrete than a caller dialing the wrong number.

"I am going to take Itty Bitty to the store with me. I need to make sure you all have some groceries while I am gone. Are you okay?"

"Um, yeah. Why?"

"You're sweating on your forehead and along your underarms."

Juan glanced down at his white t-shirt. Sure enough, he was perspiring profusely.

"Yeah, I'm okay. I was doing push-ups upstairs and had to sprint down here to answer the phone. I got to get back in shape," Juan said.

"Okay. Can I fix you some water?"

"No. I am fine."

Peyton hugged Juan. It took every piece of him not to recoil from her touch. How many other men had she hugged like that?

"Take your time, honey. I have some work to wrap up."

After Juan helped Peyton gather their daughter, he walked them to the door. He stood in the doorway while Peyton put Itty Bitty in her car seat. Once Peyton had situated herself in the driver's seat, Juan turned to go back in the house. He pushed the door closed but did not lock it. As soon as the black Maxima disappeared from view, Juan began his private investigation.

"There has to be something on the computer," Juan said.

He dashed into the computer room and turned on his computer. If there was any file or message on the computer, Juan Suarez had the ability to retrieve it.

4:00 p.m.

As Shelby parked at the mailbox in her mother's cul-de-sac, she could hear a tiny voice drifting on a lovely melody through her lowered windows. The voice belonged to Mrs. Ellen who sat on her porch singing "This Little Light of Mine" while shucking peas. Shelby stepped out of the car and walked up the driveway past the navy blue Chrysler and to the front porch of the ranch-style house.

"This little light of mine, I'm going to let it shine…" Mrs. Ellen sang. *"Ohh, This little light of mine, I'm gonna let it shine, let it shine…"*

Shelby stepped onto the porch as Mrs. Ellen ended her song. Shelby noticed that Mrs. Ellen was still dressed comfortably in a Florida shirt and aqua blue pants.

"I am surprised you are not fishing," Shelby said.

"Hey, baby! You look so good! Come over here and give me a hug!"

Shelby could not contain her smile. She hugged the slim, middle-aged woman who had given birth to five boys and had never gone over the weight of one hundred thirty-five pounds!

"Did you just get your hair done?" Mrs. Ellen asked.

"Yes, ma'am. My sister put a perm in it for me. Your hair looks good, too," Shelby complimented.

"Shoot, this ole mess. I need to get it fixed soon before it looks like a mop! Come on in and take a load off."

"Mrs. Ellen, I do not want to hold you up. I was just in the neighborhood and my sister told me that you had asked about me."

"Shelby, I have something important to tell you. Fishing can wait," Mrs. Ellen said.

Mrs. Ellen opened the front door and Shelby followed her inside. They walked past a wall of portraits and took a step down into the den that had a glass patio door. Beams of sunlight streamed through the glass door and fell on the hardwood floor. Shelby sat on a brown leather couch while Mrs. Ellen sat across from her on a recliner. The house was as quiet as a mouse.

"Where is everyone?" Shelby asked.

"Scottie, my youngest boy, is in New Orleans for the football game and the other four are with their friends today. Steve just went to the store," Mrs. Ellen explained.

"Oh, okay," Shelby said.

"Do you have any idea why I wanted to see you, Shelby?"

"Um. Probably since I haven't seen you in a long time," Shelby said.

As Mrs. Ellen smiled, her gold-trimmed left canine twinkled.

"Shelby, do you remember when you were a kid and how you would lose things and could not find them? Do you 'member how I would help you find those things that you lost?"

"Yes. I would lose jewelry and you would always help me find it the next day. I would ask if you knew magic."

"And I would tell you I was only blessed."

"Yes. I remember, but I haven't lost anything lately."

"It would seem, but I have other news. Only this time, what has slipped from your hands, you may not want back," Mrs. Ellen advised.

With that comment, Shelby leaned forward. The serious look on Mrs. Ellen's face troubled her.

"Mrs. Ellen, what are you talking about?"

"Whenever you would lose something and would tell me about it, I would dream about finding it and that's exactly where it would be. Lately, I have been dreaming about you and your husband, Benjamin."

"What did you see in your dreams?"

Mrs. Ellen got up out of her seat and sat beside Shelby. She took

Shelby's youthful hands into her own aging ones. They could feel each other's pulse.

"Shelby, I was in Shop-Mart the day before Thanksgiving and I saw your husband with another woman."

"Impossible. He was closing a business deal out of town on that day!"

Mrs. Ellen shook her hand and tightened her grip on Shelby's hand.

"They were doing some last minute shopping for Thanksgiving dinner and she was pregnant. I would give her about six months by the way she was showing."

"Noo!"

Shelby burst into tears. Her body trembled as her emotions ranged between love and hate. Mrs. Ellen hugged her tightly. Shelby's tears soaked Mrs. Ellen's shirt.

"A-are y-you sure?" Shelby sobbed.

"As sure as when you lost your pink ice ring when you were eleven years old," Mrs. Ellen replied.

"Maybe you didn't see what you thought you saw. It could have been someone he was helping."

"Shelby, I know what I saw. They were acting very much like a couple in love and they were kissing like lovers do. Benjamin was rubbing her belly like a proud father would do."

"I-I can't believe this! That bastard!"

Mrs. Ellen got up from her seat and returned with a wad of tissue for Shelby to blow her nose.

"The Lord led me to the grocery store that day. Just as I picked up some sugar, they were a couple of feet away from me. Benjamin has never met me but I have seen pictures of him at your mother's house."

"I don't doubt what you saw. I can't believe what Benjamin has done to our family!"

"Shelby, whatever is done in the dark will come to the light. Now, it is up to you on how to handle it. Do not worry. No one in this house or your mother's house will know about this conversation. This is our little secret."

"Th-thank you. I will handle it. I promise. I was supposed to go out tonight but I don't think I will. Thank you, Mrs. Ellen."

"Anytime, baby. You and your sisters are like my granddaughters. I would do anything for you. If you need me, I am only a phone call away."

"Yes, ma'am. Thank you again."

The two women hugged one final time and Mrs. Ellen walked Shelby to her car. Mrs. Ellen waved goodbye as Shelby drove down the hill.

Lord, please watch over her and don't let her do anything crazy to that man or herself, Mrs. Ellen prayed.

She popped the trunk of her blue four-door Chrysler Sedan. In the trunk was a suite of fishing poles, a fishing basket, a folding chair, and a box of tackle. She stared at the fishing gear when a thought came to her.

Relationships are like fishing. Sometimes, you catch a keeper; sometimes, you may just end up with something you have to throw back.

5:00 p.m.

Jack rode southbound on Interstate 400 toward his destination. About thirty minutes earlier, he had stopped at a phone booth in Silver City and looked up Peyton's name and address in the phone book. He had dialed the number and just breathed on the phone mafia-style. Instead of Peyton answering, her husband had answered. He sounded like a geek with an accent! Now, Jack reflected on the first line of the letter Peyton had written him five months ago.

Itty Bitty is going to have a new daddy. A daddy who is a software designer who is featured in magazines...

"Peyton, I am going to make you and Señor Suarez suffer for taking my baby from me," Jack said.

He concentrated on the road. Soon, a sign that read 'Alpharetta half a mile' came into view. He exited the ramp and stopped at the first gas station. He parked his TransAm next to a gas pump and walked into the station to pay for twenty dollars worth of gas. A friendly Pakistani clerk greeted him.

"Hello, my friend."

"Greetings. I need twenty on pump eight," Jack said pleasantly.

"Twenty dollars on pump eight, it is."

He took Jack's money and rang up the register. As the receipt printed, the store clerk noticed that Jack looked as if he had not slept in a couple of days. His eyes were bloodshot and he carried a bad body odor.

"Are you traveling far, my friend?"

"Not too far, now that you mentioned it? Are you familiar with the area?"

"Sure, I was born and raised here."

Yeah, right, and I am from the city where you need a boat instead of a car, Jack thought.

"I hate to admit it, but I am a little lost. I am on my way to visit a cousin who just moved here and thought I would surprise him for the holiday weekend," Jack said.

"Oh, I see."

"I had to work a double yesterday and didn't even get to take a shower or rest."

"I could help you, my friend. Do you have an address?"

Jack fished into his pocket and extracted a crinkled piece of paper.

"Umm, 42339 Echelon Drive. If you could help me out with how to get here, I would greatly appreciate it."

"Certainly, my friend!"

The store clerk took the crinkled paper into a back room. He returned shortly with directions from the gas station to the address provided.

"The internet is amazing. I hope this helps you, my friend," the store clerk said.

Jack glanced at the directions. The estimated time of arrival was thirty minutes.

"Thank you! My cousin is going to be so surprised when he sees me! God bless Pakistan and America," Jack said.

The store clerk was elated.

"There are not that many nice young men in the world."

Jack finished pumping his gas. Within thirty minutes, he turned onto Peyton's street. He rode up the street and scoped out the location. Peyton's house was the first brick home on the right.

"Daddy's coming home tonight," Jack said.

He made a u-turn and drove back the way he came. He parked his car at the nearby clubhouse and watched the fiery sunset.

"This is it, Jack! It's show time," he whispered to himself.

He loaded his handguns, strapped his Rambo knife to his waist, and placed a roll of duct-tape in one of his pockets. Night had fallen on Alpharetta. A murder was about to take place.

6:00 p.m.

As Peyton pulled into the grocery store's parking lot, her cell phone rang. She glanced at the caller ID. Her love was calling her. She answered the phone in a soft sexy voice.

"Hey, sweetie!"

The caller answered in a deep voice, "Baby, while I was standing here on this Creole balcony, watching the tourists walk to Bourbon Street, guess what I was thinking of?"

"Ooh, tell your gal what you were thinking of?"

"Rubbing your body down with baby oil and giving you a personal massage with my mouth."

"Ooooh! You know what a gal likes!"

"I couldn't wait to hear from you so I called your house, but your husband answered the phone."

Peyton gasped as her heart raced beneath her blouse.

"Boy, is you stupid? What did he say?"

"Be easy, my breezy. I told him I had the wrong number. He didn't suspect anything. Trust me."

Peyton calmed down. If things had been amiss, Juan would have blown up her cell phone by now.

"Byron, you can't call me on the house number!"

"Shhh. Listen. This is the song I want playing when we are making love."

Peyton listened. It was the popular song "Slow Jamz".

"Byron, I talked to Tomeka yesterday and she said that you all may be getting back together," Peyton said.

"Yeah, we are going to get back together when the white house turns black. I have to tell her things like that to keep her from trying to take all of my money," Byron said.

"Well, I guess, when you are the highest paid football player, you have to secure your finances."

"I am going to pick you up in my color changing Bentley and bring you to the Hotel Royal of New Orleans. I am going to have flowers, chocolate strawberries, and chilled champagne."

"We will see."

"Peyton, I can't wait to see you."

"You are making me melt, Byron."

"Only in my mouth and not in my hands."

"Go practice or something! I am about to go into the grocery store. I will call you later."

"Alright, love. Talk to you later."

After the phone call ended, Peyton sat in her car for a moment and reflected upon the last time they were together.

"Oooh! I can't wait to be held by those rock hard arms," Peyton shouted in the car.

Behind her, Itty Bitty played with her baby rattle. She was too young to be aware of her mother's deceitful ways.

6:15 p.m.

Jack stood on the front porch of the Suarez home and was about to kick the door open when a simple thought occurred to him. *Check the door. I'll bet it's unlocked...*

Jack heeded his criminal conscience. He gently placed his hand on the doorknob and rotated it to the right. The door opened. Jack stepped inside the foyer of the home. He left the door slightly ajar.

"As easy as one, two, three," Jack whispered.

He entered the foyer and froze when he heard tapping. He listened and crept around the corner. Juan Suarez was typing at his computer keyboard. Something had him highly upset.

"This is the jackpot! Password changed," Juan shouted.

He had just changed the password to a folder on Peyton's profile.

"Let's see what my Peyton has been hiding."

He scanned through the e-mails. They were all from a person named Byron Smith.

"That name sounds familiar."

Then, it dawned on him. Byron Smith was the highest paid football player in the league and the father of Tomeka's daughter!

"I married a whore! She is going to New Orleans to see Byron! Let me print this out!"

The printer spat out sheets of paper. The subjects of two read 'you went deep into my end-zone last night' and 'your stiff arm was tremendous'. Juan typed faster on the computer as he searched for divorce attorneys in the area. Suddenly, a red dot appeared on the computer screen.

"What in the—"

"Hell," Jack finished.

The red dot leapt from the computer screen to Juan's forehead. Suddenly, another dot leapt onto Juan's groin area. Juan could only sit in his computer chair and stare at the intruder.

"Please, don't shoot me!"

"It depends on if you tell me what I want to know."

"I don't k-eep any money here."

"Shut up and don't scream, Señor Suarez!"

Jack put away one of the pistols, stooped down, and read one of the sheets of paper:

> *Byron,*
> *I never made love in the shower.*
> *It is the closest thing to making love in the rain.*

"She cheated on you just like she cheated on me! Don't you know you can't turn a hoe into a housewife?"

"Wh-what are you talking a-about?"

"You know damn well what I am talking about, Señor Suarez! I am Peyton's ex-husband and Itty Bitty's dad!"

"I—"

"Shut up and open your mouth!"

Juan resisted. Jack kicked Juan's chair, knocking him to the floor. Before he could scream, Jack kicked Juan in the mouth. Blood and teeth spewed from his bashed mouth.

"Open your mouth!"

Juan opened his bloody mouth as he stared down the barrel of the gun. He caught the faint glimpse of the curvature of the bullet. Jack thrust the gun inside Juan's mouth.

"Disobey me again and you will need a brain transplant instead of a partial plate! Now stand up and take me to your laundry room!"

Juan slowly rose to his feet. Tears trickled down his cheeks. He carefully walked backwards as he led Jack to the laundry room. Things did not look good for Juan. It seemed that it would soon be over for him.

7:00 p.m.

Peyton's black Maxima quietly pulled into her driveway. She turned off the ignition to her car, unbuckled her seat belt, and got Itty Bitty out of her car seat. Once she had closed all the car doors, she popped the trunk so that Juan could get the groceries.

"It's almost time to go to the club," Peyton said as she glanced at her watch.

She walked to the front door of her townhouse and found the door slightly ajar.

"This guy is so lazy!"

Peyton walked into her home and left the door open for Juan. The house was strangely quiet.

"Juan, I am back with the groceries! You left the door unlocked," Peyton announced.

She bent down and put her daughter into her little swing. As she regained her posture, a rough hand tightly gripped her left shoulder and something hard pressed against the back of her head.

"If you scream, this gun will go off!"

"T-take whatever you want and j-just leave.

"What I came for is worth more than anything in this place you call home!"

"W-what do you want?"

"I want to hold my daughter before I kill you."

"Jack?"

"That's right. Jack is back!"

"Jack…you can't be here…you are supposed to be locked up."

"It is what it is. My street-smart cousin knows the judge and the district attorney. Since they both owed my cousin a favor, they took what was supposed and made it what it is!"

"You are disgusting!"

"Come on to the laundry room. I think you just pissed yourself!" Jack nudged Peyton to the laundry room.

Oh God! Please don't let Juan be dead. Peyton prayed as she shuffled forward.

Tears streamed down her face and her body trembled as thoughts of what Jack was capable of doing to her and her family wildly manifested in her head.

"J-jack, wh-whatever you do, please do not hurt Itty Bitty," Peyton pleaded.

Jack whirled Peyton around and slapped her with an open palm. "Ahh!"

"Do you actually think I would hurt my own flesh and blood!?"

Before she could answer, he backhanded her again and shoved her across the hardwood floor. Peyton felt her cell phone press against her hip. In desperation, she pressed down on all the keys, hoping that the emergency key was triggered. Peyton's vision was blurred. She rubbed her eyes and her vision quickly improved. She glanced around the laundry room. Juan was lying on his side. His legs and arms were bound in duct tape. His mouth was gagged with a dirty sock.

"Don't worry, darling! I have something special for you. After I tie you up, I am going to drop a hot steamy load into a pair of your socks and stuff it into your mouth!"

"No! No! Please! I am begging you! Please don't!"

"Shut up and tie up!"

Jack pitched a bundle of duct tape at her head. She shifted her head to the left too late.

Pain flashed across her head and a trickle of blood dripped down her face.

"Please!"

"Save it for Señor Suarez!"

"Somebody! Anybody!"

"Your husband did his homework!"

"Someone help me! Help me!"

"Peyton, guess what?"

"You're crazy! You're a maniac!"

"Your husband knows about Byron Smith laying more pipe to his wife than a plumber to a broken sink!"

"Noooo!"

"Crying ain't gonna fix anything, you slut bucket! Señor Suarez, since you are tied up, I am gonna pistol whip the snot out of this trash heap!"

"Stay away! Stay away from me," Peyton yelled.

Peyton scurried to the far corner of the room where Juan cringed. Jack slowly walked toward Peyton with the butt of his gun extended.

"Brace yourself, cutie. This may hurt," Jack said as pulled the butt of the pistol back.

BLAM!

Peyton's eyes flung open as a loud blast echoed throughout the house.

"Ahhh!" Jack yelled.

He had been shot in the arm. He spun around to see a member of the SWAT team crouching in the living room. Itty Bitty was gone from her swing and a small string of smoke rose from the barrel of the SWAT member's assault rifle.

"You sapsucka!"

Jack drew his other pistol and fired at the law enforcement agent. The SWAT member dove to his left behind a wall. Chunks of the wall were blasted away.

"You have to do better than that if you are gonna take out Jack!"

Suddenly, twenty red dots appeared on Jack's chest from the approaching SWAT team members.

"If I go, they go," Jack yelled.

He pointed right and left at Peyton and Juan.

"No!" Peyton screamed.

BLAM! BLAM!

In response, the SWAT team opened fire on Jack. The bullets knocked Jack from his feet and into a nearby glass cabinet. Peyton checked herself.

"He missed me!"

She glanced at Juan. Unfortunately, Juan was struck in the lower left side of his abdomen.

"Juan!"

The sight of Juan bleeding caused Peyton to pass out. The SWAT team secured the room and made way for the paramedics. Hopefully, they could save Juan.

8:00 p.m.

Shelby sat upstairs and stared out the window. The television was on a local station but she did not pay it any attention. On the floor, there was a small picture of an attractive black lady and a pair of pink thongs that she had found in a locked file cabinet. That cabinet was supposed to house financial documents.

"Who are you and why did you break up my family?" Shelby asked the picture.

The strong smell of bleach drifted down the hallway from the master bathroom. After she made the discovery, Shelby poured bleach into the sinks, toilet, and tub; she filled them with Benjamin's clothes. Then, she called her husband and left an urgent message on his voicemail.

"Benjamin, I need you to meet me at the house, Alexander is throwing up everything that goes down!"

Suddenly, a news flash came across the screen and snapped Shelby back to reality.

"Breaking news, a home invasion turns deadly in Alpharetta. One dead, two injured. Stay tuned."

There was the sound of a car entering the driveway. Shelby turned the television off as Benjamin parked his aqua green Mercedes Benz next to her white one.

"Benjamin, I hope God has mercy on us both," Shelby said as she hurried downstairs.

Benjamin, dressed in his dark blue slacks along with a gold silk shirt, exited his vehicle. He coolly trotted to the front door and put his key in the lock, but Shelby opened the door for him.

"What is up, baby? What's going on with Alexander?" Benjamin asked.

BANG!

"Damn, Shelby! Why don't you slam the door harder and knock all the pictures down!"

"Sometimes, I don't know my own strength."

"Well, where is Alexander? Does he have the flu or something?"

"Alexander is fine."

"What? What are you talking about? I thought you said he was sick and needed to go to the hospital! Why are you crying?"

"I told you he was sick because I needed you here. I needed you to explain this. These are not my size."

She tossed the pink thongs across the space between her and
Benjamin.

"I-I can explain."

"Explain."

"I met this lady a long time ago, before you and I—"

"Benjamin, you are such a liar!"

"Listen! Listen! It was just a fling. I would never jeopardize my
family!"

"Benjamin, I know that she is pregnant and you are the father!"

Benjamin dropped his head.

"She is eight months. It's a boy."

"I hate you so much right now! Ahhhh!"

Rage overthrew Shelby's cool demeanor. She sprinted toward
Benjamin and swung with an overhand right that was as quick as a
flash. The kickboxing classes were finally paying off.

"Ouch! You busted my lip," Benjamin yelled.

"I am gonna do more than bust your lip! I am gonna bust your
ass!"

She tried to punch him again but missed. Benjamin grabbed her
by the arm. Shelby kicked him in the knee. She felt his kneecap
shift to the left.

"My knee! You bitch!"

Shelby spun around and delivered a powerful roundhouse kick
to Benjamin's ribs. She heard a cracking sound. Then, Benjamin
collapsed on the ground.

"I want you out! I want you out! Go back to your pregnant
mistress! I am sure her swollen feet need massaging!"

"T-this is my house. *You* leave!"

Benjamin moaned as he slowly rose to his feet.

"What? You knock up some bimbo and I am supposed to leave my home! I am the mother of your children!"

"You're a lousy mother who has spoiled the kids. I don't want you or them!"

"You bastard!"

"You don't excite me! That's why I don't have sex—"

"Stay right there, Benjamin! I'm gonna cut you like a fish!"

Shelby dashed into the nearby kitchen and grabbed a butcher's knife.

"Shit!"

Benjamin limped out of the door. He hopped into his Mercedes and sped away just as Shelby made it to the doorway.

"Don't come back!"

Shelby walked back inside. She knew that she would need the best attorney that Benjamin's money could buy. She also knew that she had to think of a white lie to tell Tomeka. She was not going to the club tonight.

8:30 p.m.

Antone yawned as he awoke from his evening nap. He scooted to the edge of his bed and rubbed the sleep from his eyes. He checked the clock on his dresser. In large red numbers, the time blinked off and on.

"Must have had a power outage," Antone said. "Well, it's going to take more than a power outage to keep me from being all over Ms. Sameka Edwards tonight! Let's see what's on TV."

Antone pressed the oval power button on his remote control. He scanned through a couple of stations. He stopped on channel eight when he saw a horrifying headline describing a deadly home invasion in Alpharetta. After listening to a little of April the Anchorwoman's report, Antone turned the television off and put on his tank top and sweat pants. He walked over to his closet and extracted his newly purchased beige Stacey Adams suit. Antone walked into the hallway. Mike was still lying on the couch watching TV.

"Some things never change," Antone said.

"Hell must have frozen over! It's Friday night and you are still home!"

"The night is still young, my brother!"

"When your heart is broken, nights become long and the days become short."

"One thing I've learned is that when you are down, there is only one way to go—up."

At that moment, Gabriel came around the corner. He purposely bumped shoulders with Antone and knocked him into the wall. Antone dipped his shoulder and shoved Gabriel in the back.

"Ops, did I do that?" Antone asked sarcastically.

Before the confrontation escalated any further, Mike intervened from the couch.

"Y'all cut that out! No playing in the house! Don't make me get off of this couch!"

Antone smiled and went into the bathroom. He hung his outfit on the door, washed his face, and sung while brushing his teeth.

"Ou wemind me of my seep, I swont to wide its!"

Before he could continue his solo, Gabriel lightly knocked on the door.

"Telephone!"

Antone finished brushing his teeth and rinsed his mouth out.

"Who is it?"

"Walt," Gabriel replied.

Antone opened the door and Gabriel gave him the phone without any hassles, pushing, or name-calling.

"What it do, pimp juice?" Antone said into the phone's mouthpiece.

He slid the plastic covering off his new suit.

"Tone, I was just calling to give you some of my mojo before you went to the Caribbean."

"Thank you for your blessing, Godfather! I will not disappoint."

"Well, hit me up later on, big timer! I am out."

Antone ended the phone call and finished getting dressed. When he exited the bathroom, he was dressed to kill in a beige suit, dark brown dress shirt, matching tie, and hat.

"You look like a don," Gabriel said.

"And I feel like one, too!"

"You look like a clown!" Mike said.

"I'm bad, you know it!"

Imitating the legendary King of Pop, Antone spun around and gripped his crotch. He closed the front door. Mike continued to lie on the couch. Then, he sat up on the couch.

When you are down, there is only one way to go—up, he thought.

"Gabriel!"

"Yes, sir?"

"I am leaving you pizza money. Lock up and don't let anyone in."

"Where are you going?"

"I am going out! Tonight, Mike hits the streets of Atlanta!"

Mike leapt from the couch with a new outlook on life. He rushed to his closet and put together an outfit. From this day forward, his days of being a couch potato were over!

9:00 p.m.

Tomeka was dressed only in black lingerie when her phone rang. On her bed was a pair of jeans and an acute spaghetti strap top. The name "Shelby Harrington" pulsated on the blue flashing LCD.

"What's up, girl?"

"Hon, I am in my car going to get some salt to make some ice cream with my sisters," Shelby lied.

"Okay, so you are not going out tonight?"

"Nah, Mom made a blackberry pie, the kids are having fun with their cousins, and I may end up spending the night tonight. You know how these deer are in the country."

"I feel you on that. Family time is the best time."

"Thanks. I knew you would understand."

"Tell your mom, your sisters, and Benjamin I said hello."

The name of her husband caused Shelby to get choked up.

"Are you okay, Shelby?" Tomeka asked.

"Y-yeah. I swallowed and it went down the wrong hole."

"Well, I will make sure I have a drink for you. Call me tomorrow and I will give you the play-by-play," Tomeka said.

"I will. Tomeka?"

"Yeah?"

"Forget what I said earlier about yin and yang being balanced stuff. Get on the dance floor, strut your stuff, and make those men's hearts throb! You have so much potential! Don't let Antone or anyone tell you less!"

"I won't," Tomeka said.

"Thank you. Bye, hon."

"Bye, Shelby."

A smile formed on Tomeka's face as she ended the phone call. She knew Shelby was hiding something from her but tonight was not the night to find out. Perhaps, tomorrow Shelby would be more open to discussion. That night, Tomeka would take Shelby's advice.

"Alright, girl, let's pull out the eye catching stuff!"

She fished through her walk-in closet and pulled out a pair of three-quarter-length flared jeans. After she slipped them on, she took a look at herself in her full-body mirror. Her hair flowed down her back. The dark lines of her African tribal tattoo were visible on the small of her back.

"Beyonce, you have C.O.M.P.E.T.I.T.I.O.N!" Tomeka shouted.

She reached into the closet and pulled out a brown logo tee that had a screen print of pink letters provocatively asking, "Got D?". Then, Tomeka slipped on a pair of expensive pink and white wedge sandals with rhinestone studded straps.

"Since I will be hunting, I want my jewelry to reflect my attitude," Tomeka said.

Next, she accessed her jewelry box and pulled out her panther collection. Tomeka walked back to her mirror and stared at herself. In her ears, she wore a pair of white gold pave diamond panther earrings. On her neck, she wore a necklace with multiple panthers in a powerful stride. Their eyes were green emeralds and their spots were pink sapphires. Beneath each of these panthers was a smooth pearl.

"My darrling, you look maggnificent! My darrling! Rrrrgh," Tomeka purred in the mirror.

Next, Tomeka accessed her bracelets and watches. She chose two seven-inch diamond bracelets. She placed one on her left wrist and the other around her right ankle. Last, Tomeka pulled out a luxury timepiece that had a white mother of pearl dial set with diamonds and a bezel set with pink sapphires.

"I'm so icy! Icy! Icy," Tomeka sang as she modeled in the mirror.

She left the mirror. Then, she picked up her blue clutch purse and car keys from the dresser. Tomeka placed a pair of pink and platinum sunglasses on her forehead and wiped a coat of shiny watermelon lip-gloss across her lips.

"Girl, you are going to make someone catch the Holy Ghost tonight!"

Tomeka sprayed her neck and clothing with a tempting fragrance before she exited her condo. She took the elevator to the floor level where she passed the security guard's desk.

The on-duty guard shouted out a compliment, "Somebody call the Atlanta Fire Department because you are on fire!"

"Thanks. Keep my building safe!"

She walked to where her truck was parked and hopped in. She turned on the ignition and checked the time on her dashboard display. It was 10:00 p.m. and she had not heard from Peyton. She pulled out of the parking deck and called Peyton. Upon the first ring, Tomeka's phone call was directed to Peyton's voicemail.

"Thank you for calling but as you can see I am not available. Please leave your name and number and I will return your phone call."

Tomeka ended the phone call.

"Ain't this a 'B'? First, Shelby; now, Peyton! If they didn't want to go out that is all they had to say!"

Tomeka had a second thought and called back. This time, she left Peyton a message.

"Peyton, it is a little after ten o'clock and I am on my way to the IHOP where we're supposed to meet. Call me back when you get this message. Bye."

Tomeka proceeded as planned. Hopefully, Peyton would be waiting for her.

10:30 p.m.

Two young men, Randy and Tony, walked down a concrete path that was bordered by torches and blow-up palm trees. Randy sported crisscrossing braids and Tony had a low fade. They passed a long line of men and women, dressed to impress, patiently waiting to enter the extravagant nightclub called Caribbean Nights.

"I can't believe the e-mail line is wrapped around to the valet parking lot," Tony exclaimed.

"We should have been in line at 9:30 p.m., kinfolk," Randy said.

"Did you see that redbone with the short hair in the red fishnet shirt?"

"Yes! What about the dreadhead with the tight black catsuit," Randy asked.

"Nah, I didn't see her. What did she look like?"

"Kinfolk, she was awesome! I would go to church with her!"

"Man, you need to go to church for another reason besides a girl who wears a catsuit to the club!"

"Yeah, you're right. I heard the owner spent a cold million on this place," Randy said.

"It used to be a coffee bistro. I think the newspaper said that it is twenty thousand square feet, three bars, and glass VIP rooms with blue and pink lights flashing everywhere," Tony said.

"A friend of my cousin named 3-2 works here as a bouncer."

"Why do they call him 3-2?

"When he played defensive tackle in college, no one could block him. He started calling himself 3-2 because three always beats two! There is no competition!"

"Dang! Did he go to the league?"

"Nawh. He got hurt, but he said whenever there is fight they toss the guys out like in the movies," Randy said.

"You mean by the back of their pants?"

"Yep!"

"Well, let's get into this line so we can see the limelight!"

They walked toward the shorter line that required a twenty-dollar fee to get in the extravagant nightclub. At that time, Antone's white car pulled into the driveway of the valet parking lot. The crowd had started to bounce. They cranked their wrists back and forward like a motorcycle to the sounds of the Atlanta classic, "It's Going Down!"

"Meet me in the Club! It's going down..."

The valet personnel sprinted toward Antone's car. As he approached, Antone popped the top to his gray armrest. He reached inside, grabbed the VIP card Sameka had given him, and held it out the window.

"Good evening, monsieur," the valet personnel greeted.

"Here's my card. I am VIP," Antone replied.

The valet took the card and read it. Then, he gave it back to Antone.

"VIP is fifty dollars to park, monsieur."

"But my card—"

"Your card is for a free disposable camera at Shop-Mart."

Antone jerked the card away from the valet personnel and read it. This was the card that he was supposed to have given the lady who tried to run him over! He had given away the wrong card! Antone banged his head against his steering wheel.

"Will you be parking, monsieur?" the valet personnel asked.

"Did I hear you correctly? You did say fifty dollars to park?"

"Qui."

"We...there is no we. I don't know you."

"Qui."

"Look, man, I am not for that foot tapping in the bathroom!"

"Qui is French for yes!"

"I don't like your tone. Where is your supervisor?"

"Monsieur, it is fifty to park."

"I don't like your service, Jarret," Antone said as he read the valet personnel's nametag.

"Monsieur..."

"Supervisor! I want your supervisor!"

A line of cars had formed behind Antone's car. Jarret looked around then leaned forward.

"How much?" Jarret asked.

"Ten. Take it or leave it," Antone said.

"Twenty."

"Fifteen."

BEEP!

"Quit kissing and park the car," a driver yelled two cars behind Antone.

Antone quickly fished out a ten and a five dollar bill.

"Fifteen," Antone said.

"Done."

Jarret opened the car door. Antone stepped out of his car. Jarret quickly parked Antone's car in the front and handed him his keys. Antone activated the car's alarm as he walked toward the end of the twenty-dollar line and addressed the ladies as he passed.

"What's up, ladies?"

That didn't work, but Antone kept it rolling.

"Hold a dance for me, girl."

"Alright," a woman replied.

Antone tipped his hat at the woman and walked down the line. He started dancing in front of a group of women.

"Meet me at the bar, it's going down!"

They danced with him. Antone walked to the end of the line. The night was his. As he stood in line, Antone listened to the general conversation that surrounded him.

"The money you pay for rent could be used to pay on a 30-year mortgage," one guy said to another.

"Girl, heavy eyeliner makes you look slutty. Now, it's cool if that is what you and your man is into but it's not cool for a job interview," a woman said to her female friends.

However, one conversation that involved three women caught his attention. He listened and profiled the three divas: KeKe, Michelle, and Fancy.

"Note to self: KeKe is classy but definitely from the hood," Antone said to himself.

KeKe was the shortest of the group and wore a pink halter dress with blue four-inch heels. She had a short bouncy flip hairstyle that was streaked in light pink highlights. She wore hot pink lipstick with blazing blue eye shadow. She had a south Atlanta drawl. Her two upper canines were gold.

"Note to self: Michelle is the professional. She probably works in one of the skyscrapers on Peachtree Street."

Michelle had long jet-black hair and a short pointy nose. Michelle's attire consisted of a silver suit and a camisole. She did not wear any make-up.

"Note to self: Fancy is the Don Datta! Do not cross her!"

Fancy wore a sparkling tiara and a black dress with a square neckline. Fancy's hair was in micro-braids. Even more stunning than her appearance was her Jamaican tongue. Antone listened closer and discovered that all three of the women shared one characteristic: They had all met the same man here, provided him with their numbers, and never received a phone call from him. Tonight, all three were hoping to see him again.

"Shawty, you can tell how he wear his clothes that he got some big muscles," said KeKe. "He could pick up me and all my problems!"

"Lil dirty sang 'Drifting on a Memory' one day. I thought I was on the front row of a concert," Michelle said.

"John Wane is a real man who does real tings. Two tings you never forget about a real man—you never forget his name or where you met him," Fancy said.

"Note to self: John Wane is a pimp! He never called these women and they still like him!"

Antone had heard enough. He introduced himself.

"Good evening. I couldn't help but overhear your conversation. My name is Antone Wright."

"Well, Mr. Wright, talk to us inside the club when we are thirsty," Michelle said.

"I just wanted to tell you that, although, I am the new kid on the block, this John Wane has nothing on me."

"Shawty, I don't know who has been pumping yo' head up with regular unleaded but you ain't got nothing on John Wane" KeKe said.

"Look-a-herr, Jake nicca. The line is moving so mind ya business," Michelle interjected.

"Point taken," Antone said.

A few minutes later, Antone showed his driver's license to the security guard and walked inside. If he could not find Sameka, he would make sure he found someone of equal value. He walked into the club and felt as if he was in a win-win situation. Or so he thought.

11:00 p.m.

Tomeka called Peyton again. The result was still the same.

"Thank you for calling but as you can see I am not available. Please leave your name and number and I will return your phone call."

Tomeka bit her bottom lip in frustration. Peyton and Shelby had stood her up. The night was supposed to have been one of glamour. She hoped it wouldn't be a total disaster. She looked into her rearview mirror and made a decision.

"I'm going to the club by myself!"

She shifted her truck into gear, pulled out of the parking lot, and on to Peachtree Street. She traveled until a red light stopped her at the intersection of Tenth Street. At that moment, a black Expedition full of handsome black men with cornrows, necklaces, and urban gear pulled up beside her. Tomeka studied the driver. He had full lips, long eye lashes, and a neatly trimmed beard. The guy was not

Denzel, but he was far from ug-mo, which is short for ugly plus more.

"I wonder if he knows how to use his lips," Tomeka pondered to herself. *I think I will get the party started and get them digits!*

"Hey, hon," the driver said.

"What's up?" Tomeka replied.

Tomeka studied him a little deeper. The driver had a deep voice with a touch of northern exposure. There could be potential.

"Can we get over, sweetie? I am trying to beat the crowd."

Tomeka blinked in disbelief. The driver pointed to the gay club on Tomeka's left. The line into the front and back of the club was teeming with men. Tomeka quickly cut her losses and beckoned for them to get over.

"Go ahead. Good hunting!"

As the light turned green, the black Expedition pulled out in front of her truck and pulled into the gay nightclub. Tomeka continued her journey at full speed ahead. She soon saw a line going into Caribbean Nights.

"Man, I hope my hook-up is not bootleg!"

She slowed up and cruised into the valet parking of the fabulous Caribbean Nights. One of the valet personnel quickly approached her. Once he was there, he opened the door of her vehicle.

"Bienvenue, Mademoiselle."

Tomeka glanced at the valet's nametag and addressed him in French.

"Comment ça va, Jarret?"

"Huh?"

"You said welcome, so I asked how you were. So, how are you?"

"Oh. I am sorry. My French isn't that good. I am fine."

Suddenly, Tomeka gasped and placed her hand on her chest. Jarret saw the surprised look on her face.

"Are you okay? You look as if you just saw a ghost."

"That white car in the front belongs to my ex-boyfriend. Can you place my car in the back away from that heap?"

"Sure that will be sixty dollars," Jarret said.

"John Wane told me that you would take care of me."

At the mention of John Wane, Jarret straightened his posture.

"Yes! I sure will. The VIP line is right over there under the archway where those two big guys are standing. Give me one moment to park your car."

Jarret drove off and returned with her keys.

"Enjoy your night."

"Thank you and I will."

Tomeka strutted toward the archway of the VIP section where two security guards stood shoulder-to-shoulder. The two security guards were dressed in black suits, black shades, and had state of the art earpieces with microphones on their heads. The security guard on the left was a brown-skinned guy with a baldhead named Cedrick. The security guard on the right was a light-skinned guy who wore his hair in a 70's afro named Fredrick. As Tomeka neared, the men whispered.

"Here comes a bopper," Cedrick, the security guard with the baldhead, said.

"She has a cute face and a slim waist," Fredrick, the security guard with the afro, said.

"She is finer than the one last week."

"Man, look at those two midgets bouncing in her shirt! Oh, my God!"

"Let's see if she has a bone in her neck," Fredrick said.

"Is this the entrance to the V.I P?" Tomeka asked.

"Depends," Fredrick said.

"Depends on what?"

"It depends on whether or not you are on the VIP list," Cedrick answered.

"And if I am not?"

The two men smiled. Tomeka knew exactly what those smiles meant. Those smiles were reserved for shallow-minded groupies who would trade something precious for something of no value.

"If you are not on the list, then you have to go to that long line where it is twenty dollars to get in," Fredrick informed.

"Or you can get with the Marta," Cedrick said.

"The Marta…what's that?"

"You know the A-Train," Fredrick said.

"Umm! I never heard of it."

"The two on one fast break or the ménage-a-trios," Cedrick said.

"Oh, that! I know what you are talking about now!"

"So, is that a yes?"

Baldheaded Cedrick became hyped. This was what he had taken the job for. However, Tomeka was too woman-like and clever.

"Sorry, boys, but John Wane invited me and told me to see Britney."

There was a drastic change in the expressions on their faces at the mention of the name. They straightened up their posture and quickly offered their apologies.

"We are so sorry. Please accept our apologies," Cedrick pleaded.

"We were just joking. Umm, don't mention this to Mr. Wane," Fredrick begged.

"Apology accepted but you two need Jesus!"

Tomeka walked past the two security guards and entered a dimly lit, red-carpeted passageway. A pretty lady sat behind a booth at the end of the corridor. As Tomeka drew closer, she could feel the bass through the walls. She made it to the booth and greeted to the lady.

"Hello. Are you Britney?"

"In the flesh. Did those two overgrown kids harass you?"

"Not that much," Tomeka said.

"One day, J.W. is going to beat them at their own game."

"Do you mean John Wane?"

"Yeah, J.W. is the man around here. He is the big man who writes the checks that never bounce."

"He invited me to the club and asked me to see you."

"Ahh…Ms. Eastwood. I've been expecting you."

"How did you know it was me?"

"J.W left me a note to look out for you. Now, let me put this special green band on you. Then you can go inside."

"Huh?"

"I'm going to be honest with you, Ms. Eastwood. I've seen women look all over this club for him but he has never done this before. He must have seen something special in you."

"So, he is a player. I should have known!"

"Oh, no! J.W is a good man, a one-woman man. For him to have left specific instructions for you to find him means something. You must determine what that something special is. Now, let me have your left wrist."

Tomeka extended her left arm and Britney wrapped the florescent green band around her wrist.

"Enjoy your time, Ms. Eastwood and don't hurt him hammer!"

"I won't. Thanks, Britney."

Tomeka left Britney and walked up a narrow flight of steps. The music grew louder yet clearer. As Tomeka neared the top of the steps, she wondered, "Who is John Wane?"

11:30 p.m.

In forty-five minutes, Antone had walked around the club three times and had consumed two drinks but there was still no sign of Sameka. There were plenty of candidates for the job but he was still reserving that one interview for that special person.

"If I were Sameka, where would I go?" Antone asked himself.

There were too many possibilities. There were the glass VI.P rooms, secluded private rooms, the packed dance floor, and even the bathrooms. Antone weighed his options as pink and blue strobe lights dazzled among the indentions in the walls where exotic dancers danced in their skimpy lingerie and muscular bare-chested men posed like statues. Suddenly, Antone came to a clever solution as D.J. Silver Knight mixed Alicia Keys' smash hit, "You Don't Know My Name" behind Michael Jackson's "Rock with You".

"Well, if I can't go to you, I will have you come to me!"

Antone ran to the D.J. booth and made a special request.

"Yo! What's up playa?" Antone exclaimed.

The D.J. nodded his head. The music was too loud. Antone stepped down from the D.J booth and found a nearby table. He pulled out a pen and wrote down his plea on a napkin.

Please play "Slow Jamz" and dedicate it to Sameka from Antone. It's her birthday. Tell her to come to the D.J. booth.

Then, he leapt back up the steps to the DJ Booth and pressed the note against the glass. The DJ nodded and gave a thumbs-up sign. Antone's heart was beating hard as the music lowered and D.J. Silver Knight yelled into the microphone.

"I see you, Caribbean Nights! I know it's somebody's birthday in here! Can I get a 'hell, yeah'!"

"Hell, Yeah! Hell, Yeah!"

"Caribbean Nights, it's ya boy, D.J. Silver Knight, on the wheels of steel bringing you the trill!"

"Yeah! Yeah!"

"Caribbean Nights, I have a special dedication to a special lady from a special guy named Antone! Sameka, it's your birthday, so come down and get your birthday gift! Caribbean Nights, D.J. Silver Knight is calling everyone out to the dance floor for 'Slow Jamz'!"

"She said she wants some Marvin Gaye, some Luther Vandross, a little Anita, will definitely set this party off right…"

Jamie Foxx's suave voice resonated through the speakers
as Antone watched and waited. The VIP rooms emptied at the
command of D.J. Silver Knight.

"Where are you? Where are you? Come on!" Antone said as he
searched the immense crowd.

Antone dared not step into the grinding and two-stepping and be
swept away by its rhythmic current. Just as Twista prepared to spit
his verse, Sameka emerged from the crowd wearing a sleeveless pink
top with a matching skirt. Antone was struck by Sameka's muscular
shoulders as she pushed through the crowd. *Damn! Her arms
are more toned then mine! She must work out all the time*, Antone
thought. Crispy fives, tens, and twenty-dollar bills were pinned to
the sleeveless top and her long black silky ponytail hung loosely
over her left shoulder. The sight of this beautiful woman brightened
Antone's smile!

"Baby, drop another slow jam and all us lovers need hold hands,
and if you ain't got no man hop up on my Brougham. I keep it
pimpin' like an old man…"

"I was beginning to think you were not coming," Sameka yelled.

"Traffic on the Southside held me up," Antone replied.

"I'm glad you came. The DJ thing was very romantic."

"Hang around and I will show you the definition."

Antone seized the moment and kissed her on the cheek. They
moved to the dance floor and Antone passionately pulled Sameka
close to him. As they slowly danced, Antone could feel the magic. It
fueled his desire for Sameka.

"You have strong hands," Sameka said as they danced.

"Strong hands to hold you with."

Sameka blushed and laid her head on his chest as the sweet melody played.

"She said she wants some Marvin Gaye, some Luther Vandross, a little Anita will definitely set this party off right…"

"Your cologne is turning me on!"

"Where have you been all of my life?"

Sameka moaned. Every part of her body was tingling. What would happen if they made love?

"Antone?"

"Yes, darling."

"Is this real? Is this really happening?"

"This is as real as your job direct depositing your check in your bank every two weeks."

They stared into each other's eyes. This was ultimate. This was meant to be. Sameka lightly kissed Antone on the side of his neck with a quick touch of a wet tongue.

"Don't start the car if you're not going to drive it," Antone said.

"Not only am I going to drive it, I am going own the car."

Instantly, she felt something poke against her hip. She, however, did not recoil from human nature. She liked what Antone was packing.

She said she want some Ready for the World, some New Edition, some Minnie Riperton, and definitely set this party off right…

DJ Silver Knight mixed the upbeat reggaeton of Sean Paul's "Gimme the Light" behind "Slow Jamz". The immense crowd began to break apart. Antone and Sameka, however, remained together.

"You are a good dancer," Antone said.

"Thanks, but I can't move to this song. It's too fast."

"Well, let's go to the bar."

"Follow me. I owe you a drink, remember?"

"That's right. Lead the way."

Sameka took Antone by the hand and rubbed the inside of his palm with her finger. Antone licked his lips at the sexual sign. Sameka wanted him just as bad he wanted her. Tonight, there would be some hot love making. From across the club, in a glass VIP room, Tomeka peered at the couple. They were headed in her direction.

MIDNIGHT

When D.J. Silver Knight made the announcement about the special dedication, Tomeka had briskly run over to the glass and peered across the club. Near the DJ booth, she saw Antone and some two-bit trick dancing.

"He never danced with me! How long has he known that girl?" Tomeka murmured.

Tomeka slurped her second Cosmopolitan drink as she watched the couple dance. The announcement had caused her to send the first drink down the hatch. Now, the alcohol encouraged her anger and pushed her toward a dangerously deranged mode.

"Look at 'em grinding like there is no tomorrow!"

Tomeka finished the second Cosmopolitan and almost dropped her martini glass when she saw the couple heading to the same VIP room that she was in. For the first time, Tomeka took notice of her surroundings. On a nearby table, there were blue and red balloons with the words 'Happy Birthday'. There was a large card on the table that read: Happy Birthday, Sameka Edwards.

"Oh, my God! I have to get out! I am not ready to see Antone with another woman! I will not look like a stalker!"

Unfortunately, there was only one way in and one way out which meant Tomeka would have to pass Antone. She took a deep breath as she walked toward the exit. She gave herself some good advice.

"Tomeka, you've been drinking! Don't do anything stupid! Stay calm!"

Tomeka's mind flashed back to her dream earlier that morning. Was that a dream or a warning about tonight? Suddenly, the women at Sameka's table began to cheer!

"I see them! Here they come! Here they come!"

As Tomeka struggled to calm herself, a young man studied her actions from a safe distance at a nearby bar. The man's hazel eyes glanced at the fluorescent green wristband on the woman's wrist.

Ms. Eastwood came but something is wrong! Something is going down!

The man watched. Tonight, he would save his damsel in distress and reintroduce himself.

12:05 a.m.

Antone held Sameka's hand as they ascended the red-carpeted stairs that led into the crowded glass VIP. Suddenly, D.J. Silver Knight made a dirty south announcement.

"I want all my Down South peeps to come down to the dance floor and put your fists up and show these out-of-towners how we bust a busta's head!"

D.J. Silver Knight mixed in "We Some Head Bustas" by Lil Scrappy. This announcement caused a bottleneck effect to occur as people rushed from the VIP rooms to the dance floor.

"Do you want to go back?" Antone asked.

"No. This will give us a chance to talk in private," Sameka said.

They waded through the crowd. Antone glanced ahead of
Sameka. The three women he had met outside the club were pushing
and shoving their way through the crowd. As Sameka squeezed
through a small opening, she let go of Antone's hand.

"Antone, I'm at the bar," Sameka shouted.

"Here I come!"

At that moment, Fancy and her friends bumped into Antone.
KeKe's cup of blue vodka splattered onto her black dress. She
stopped dead in her tracks.

"Dang, Fancy! You made me spill my drink," KeKe said.

"Me, too," Michelle said.

"Cu ya u goofy doti battybwoy made you spill your drink!"
Fancy exclaimed.

They angrily stared at Antone. He looked around. It seemed
as if everyone was waiting to see how he would handle the situation.
Antone heard a guy behind him say, "He done messed up now. Mad
Jamaicans are dangerous. They will cut ya deep!"

"Folk, you might as well go on to the bar and buy us all a drink,
shawty, before we have to crank it up on you Pierre Cardin, cause
I'm from da Ville shawty and we don't play," KeKe said.

"I don't give a damn where you're from," Antone said.

"I ain't even gaggin about this Jake-nicca! Look-a-herr you lil
getter! We will get with you, dirty! I put that on my son!" Michelle
badgered.

Below them the crowd grew out of control as the DJ mixed in
another song.

"Get on my Level! Get on my Level! Get on my Level!"

Antone stood on the tip of his toes and saw Sameka. She pointed
over to a roped off section with balloons. Antone nodded his head.

At that moment, Tomeka squeezed through a small opening by the three angry women. Antone saw her standing there as beautiful as ever.

"Tomeka!" Antone yelled.

Tomeka turned toward the sound of his voice. They were only inches apart but the concept of commitment kept them miles apart. She turned her head and tried to move forward, but the crowd was gridlocked. D.J. Silver Knight had mixed in T.I.'s "Rubber Band Man" and the crowd went crazy.

"Ay, who I'm is? Rubber band man, Wild as the Taliban, 9 in my right, 45 in my other hand…"

However, Fancy was angrier than ever.

"I know you hear me talking to you, bobo! I shudda box ya in u chatta box," yelled Fancy.

"Speak English! You are in America now!"

"Go to the bar and buy us the beverages that you spilled!"

Antone ignored the angry Jamaican lady and grabbed Tomeka by her forearm.

"Get your hands off of me, Antone!"

"Tomeka…it doesn't have..."

"But it is! All I ever asked was for you to be a man and not a boy!"

"Listen—"

"You wanted to be free like a bird so I let you go! Now, let me go!"

Her words fell on deaf ears as Antone tightened his grip to force her to listen to him.

"Antone, you're hurting me!"

"Tomeka, I never wanted to be away from you. I never—"

BAM!

Fancy punched Antone on the left side of his head. The punch broke his hold on Tomeka and sent his hat flying into the crowd.

"I know that hurt!" someone shouted.

"You crazed boi! I told you I would box you in ya chatta box!"

"Stop, Antone!" Tomeka yelled.

She was too late. Antone swung an open palm at the angry Jamaican. A tall man caught Antone's hand before it made contact. He gave Antone a shove that sent him staggering backwards and into a table.

"Shawty, it's him! It's the man himself," KeKe said.

"Look-a-here! John—," Michelle started.

"Wane," Fancy finished.

Quickly, the mysterious man reached into the pocket of his black suit jacket and produced a two-way radio. Tomeka stared at the wide shoulders of the clean-cut man with a nicely trimmed dark goatee and wavy fade. He definitely was an athlete.

"This is John Wane. I am in the Glass VIP room. Level three situation. I repeat, level three situation."

"Affirmative. Three-two is en route."

"Fake-ass security guard! You are about to get your ass whooped!" Antone yelled.

Antone rushed toward John Wane but was stopped short by two large security guards. They grabbed him and slung him backwards.

"Why you—"

Antone's sentence was stopped short as more security guards entered the VIP room. They formed a barrier between their boss and Antone. Tomeka could not see through the tall security guards.

"Someone is about to get that ass kicked in the V.I.P room! This

song is for you, buddy! Sammy Sam and the Oomp Camp!" D.J.
Silver Knight exclaimed as he peered across the club toward the
glass VIP.

"Knuckle up, Boy! Knuckle up, Boy! Knuckle Up, Boy!
Knuckle up, Boy! Knuckle up, Boy! Knuckle Up, Boy!"

The security guards converged on Antone.

"Don't hurt him," Tomeka pleaded.

"Box dung dat rude bwoy spilled my drink," Fancy exclaimed.

"Here! Here's twenty dollars!"

"Tanks but I don't know why," Fancy said.

"Please, don't hurt him! Yes, he is an idiot, but please don't hurt
him! I just paid for the spilled drinks so please don't hurt him!"

John Wane heard Tomeka's plea and pulled out his radio.

"Stand down! I'm coming forward."

John Wane stepped in front of his security guards and took a
good look at Antone. Sweat stood out on his forehead, his suit was
wrinkled, and his short hair was messed up. One hand clenched an
empty champagne bottle and the other was balled up in a trembling
fist.

"Whatever your name is, please put down the bottle. I am
going to give you two choices. There will not be a third. Do you
understand?" John Wane explained.

Antone did not respond. His eyes darted from right to left. John
Wane continued to talk Antone down.

"The young lady has paid for your spilled drinks. So, here are
your choices. Stay here and enjoy the party without grabbing anyone
else by the arm or leave willingly."

"Man, fuck you!"

"I told you there would be no third choice. Three-two, toss him out!"

Three-two, the largest of the security guards, grabbed Antone by the back of his shirt and pants. He hauled Antone off his feet and carried him to the exit. Sameka grabbed her purse and followed them.

"Antone! Wait!" Sameka screamed.

The party continued as John Wane led Tomeka to a nearby table. They took a seat.

"What is he going to do to him?" Tomeka asked.

"They are going to toss him out the club. Don't worry, 3-2 won't hurt him unless I say so," John Wane said.

"I-I can't believe this is happening."

"This is what happens when I catch men harassing women in my club. I did not leave this green wristband for you to be harassed, Ms. Eastwood."

"Your voice sounds the same over the phone. What is your real name?" Tomeka asked.

"What? A black man can't be named John Wane?"

He smiled and displayed a set of even pearly white teeth and full lips.

"No, I am not saying that. I am just saying, why the alias?"

"I use the alias because I don't want everyone to know who I am."

"Oh! Are you like a vigilante crime fighter who climbs walls or something?"

John Wane laughed.

"No, of course not. I am a private man who wishes to remain private and not affect the lives of those around me."

"So considerate."

"Let me reintroduce myself. My name is Amere Destiny and I am the owner of this establishment."

"Heh! Heh!" Tomeka laughed uneasily.

"Why do you laugh?"

"I was supposed to come to the club with my friends but I end up talking to a handsome guy who had the wrong number."

"And what's wrong with that?"

"It's too easy! Too easy! I don't know where to begin."

"First, you can give me the privilege of knowing your name."

"I am so rude. I apologize. My name is Tomeka Washington."

"I am pleased to meet you."

"Tomeka Washington, thank you for coming to my party."

Amere knelt before Tomeka and kissed her hand. Already, the drama that had surrounded her that night was fading. She could manage only two words.

"Thank you."

Amere rose to his feet.

"Tomeka, I really wish I had a camera."

"Why?"

"Because you are picture perfect!"

"Thank you," she blushed.

Inside, Tomeka screamed uncontrollably.

"Do you cook?"

"Every day for me and my little girl."

"Clear your calendar because I am going to be your chef for one day."

"You cook? Please. I am not trying to be rushed to the hospital to have my stomach pumped."

"Woman, you are looking at the number one recruit for steak and shrimp! Benihana's tried to recruit me out of high school but I was like, that's okay, I'm going to college!"

"Ha! Ha! Ha!"

Tomeka was glad to see Amere had a sense of humor. She knew that she had to be wary of Amere's charm. She knew that if she wasn't careful, she would find herself becoming the victim of a one-night stand.

"Seriously speaking, I want to get to know you better. Perhaps we could schedule a date on the calendar for a candlelight dinner. We can sip on some wine, Kool Aid, or whatever is clever?"

"To be honest, Amere, I have had too much excitement tonight, but if you give me a card I would be glad to accept your dinner offer."

"Very well, I look forward to hearing from you and it was a pleasure to meet a lady as gorgeous as yourself. Have a safe drive home and thank you again for visiting Caribbean Nights, the hottest spot in Atlanta!"

Tomeka placed the card in her clutch purse and walked away. She did not have to turn around to know that Amere was still standing there watching her as she exited the VIP room. When she made it to her vehicle, she transferred the contact number to her phone. She glanced at where Antone had been parked. The spot was empty.

"Antone's loss is another's gain. I am going to call you, Amere, and I pray that you are everything that I need you to be," Tomeka said.

She pulled off and drove back to her condo. Perhaps, this relic of a good man would clean up all the mess that was in her life.

12:45am

Mike entered Caribbean Nights dressed in black shoes, navy blue slacks, and a black French collared button-down. His hair was neatly trimmed. Everything about Mike Wright was new and improved. He walked to the bar and ordered a drink.

"Hennessey and coke."

The blonde-haired female bartender went to work scooping ice and mixing cognac and coke together. In less than ten seconds, Mike had the drink of his choice.

"That's ten," the bartender said.

Mike handed the bartender a ten and a five.

"Thanks. Keep the change," Mike said.

Mike sipped his drink. It was strong. The liquor gave him courage. He stepped away from the bar and into the crowd. He walked and sipped. Before he knew it, there was only ice in his cup.

"I should have left an open tab."

He turned around to go back to the bar, and that was when he bumped into a white lady with dark hair.

"I'm sorry about that," Mike apologized.

"That's fine."

Mike took another look at the lady. He had met numerous white women, but this one was a little different. He could feel it.

"Can I ask you a question?"

"Yeah."

"Are you from here?"

"No. I am from Miami. I just moved here."

"What made you trade warm winters for cold ones?" Mike asked.

"Hurricanes. We get a hurricane every 2 years or so."

"Almost like my divorces. I am prone to meeting women who

take advantage of marriage."

"My brothers have the same problem. There are not too many good women out there anymore."

"So, are you a good woman?"

"I'm no saint but I do know how to treat my man."

Mike bit his lip. He had to give himself a chance. Lying on the couch day in and day out had provided him no chance.

"What about you? Are you from here?" the woman asked.

"Yes, born and raised."

"There aren't too many natives. Everyone moves here."

"Yeah, I know but we are still here working nine to five."

At that moment, D.J. Silver Knight mixed in "Hey, Mr. D.J" performed by R. Kelly.

Hey Mr. D. J, why don't you slow this party down. The ladies in here are fly and one just caught my eye…

Mike seized the opportunity.

"My name is Mike."

"My name is Selena."

Mike shook Selena's hand and pulled her close.

"Do you want to dance?"

"Sure, why not."

Mike tossed his cup of ice into a nearby trash can and took Selena by the waist. They danced to the music. Selena was surprised.

"Oh, you have moves! Everyone wants to bounce or grind," Selena shouted above the music.

"I am a little more seasoned than my peers," Mike said.

Mike twirled Selena. Then, he led her to the left.

"Your footwork is amazing! You haven't stepped on my feet, yet!"

"Baby, I can dance like a professional dancer and float like a butterfly," Mike said.

"Where have you been all my life?"

"On the couch watching T.V!"

Selena laughed as Mike led her to the right.

"Are you seeing anyone?"

"Why?" Mike asked.

"I want to know who the lucky person is that gets to dance with you."

"That would be Mrs. Nobody."

Selena laughed again. Mike enjoyed her laughter.

"Do you know what I am doing tomorrow?"

"Surprise me." Mike said.

"I am going to be waiting for your phone call."

Selena produced a business card.

"I won't keep you waiting long."

Mike placed the card in his pocket and continued to dance. Mike closed his eyes and enjoyed the moment. This felt much better than watching television on the couch.

2:20 am

Antone woke from his sleep. He was in Sameka's room. The lights were dim. He turned over. Sameka was lying next to him; her naked body was half covered by the sheets. Antone lifted up the sheet and spoke to his third leg. He thanked it for its performance.

"You are the man! You did that!"

Antone pulled the sheet back up and reflected on the events of the night. Sameka was the last person he had expected to see after the bouncer had tossed him out of the club. Sameka had come running out of the club to his rescue. She dared the security guard to touch him.

"If you touch him, he will sue," Sameka yelled.

Antone smiled at the memory. Sameka could be exactly what he needed in his life. She had her own money, a good job, and was a beast in the bed. Perhaps, they could go on vacation to the Bahamas or to Aruba. Antone rolled over and glanced at Sameka's dresser. He blinked and rubbed his eyes. There was a picture of a fair-skinned guy dressed in a red sweater on her dresser.

"*I knew it was too good to be true! She has a man!*"

Antone looked closer. The man looked exactly like Sameka!

"*Whew! It must be her brother. Wait. What's this?*"

Quietly, Antone glanced down and picked up a smaller photo album that was on the edge of the dresser.

"*Just to be sure...brotha don't need any surprises.*"

Antone quietly thumbed through the album.

"Here's a picture of her brother at the fair riding a merry-go-round. What type of man rides the merry-go-round with a smile on his face? Ugggh!"

Antone continued to flip through the album.

"Another one: Dude is on the beach with some super-tight Speedos on. This guy has issues and I am not talking magazines."

Antone flipped to another picture and paused.

"*Dang that car is smashed! The hood is in the trunk! How could someone live through that? Maybe her brother died?*"

He continued to thumb through the pictures. It was the last two dramatic pictures that almost made him yell out loud.

"Goodness! Someone opened a can of 'beating with a stick' on you."

A person's head was wrapped in layers of gauze. Only the eyes were visible and the sockets were swollen shut. IV's and other tubes stretched from the person's body. Antone read the caption at the bottom of the picture.

"January 23rd, 2001: Sam after car wreck…"

Antone flipped the next page. There was a picture of Sameka in the hospital bed. She had a couple of light blemishes on her face. Get Well balloons floated beside the bed.

"What in the…"

Tears formed in Antone's eyes as he read the caption under the picture.

"May 31st, 2001: Sameka, after car wreck…"

Antone wept as he slid from bed, gathered his clothes, and snuck out of the room. Sameka did not notice that he had left the bed.

"I kissed him…I kissed her…I went downtown on a he-she!"

Just as he sneaked out of Sameka's room, the hardwood floor in the hallway creaked. Sameka woke up.

"Antone, where are you, babe? I'm ready for round two."

"H to the Nawh!"

Antone sprinted down the stairs and to the front door in the split foyer. Behind him, he could hear Sameka jumping out of the bed and hurrying to the door. He fidgeted with the deadbolt lock.

"Got to get out! I am not gay!"

Sameka, wrapped in her sheet, stood at the top of the stairs.

"Antone, what are you doing?"

"I saw the pictures on your dresser!"

"Antone, that is my brother!"

"You're lying! I saw the before and after pictures in the album! You used to be a man!"

Sameka took a deep breath. There was no need to hide the truth anymore.

"Antone, that was a long time ago. I had a bad car accident. My genitals were crushed! I had no choice but to become a woman!"

Antone vomited on the floor.

"Antone, are you okay?"

"Stay away from me! You tricked me!"

"Antone, I had no choice!"

Finally, Antone unlocked the door and opened it.

"There is always a choice. Next time, give whoever you want to sleep with the choice to choose!"

Antone dashed to his car. He hopped into his car and peeled out from Sameka's front yard as he sped away.

"I can't believe this! How many people has she, I mean, he been with?"

Antone glanced at himself in his rearview mirror.

"Antone, we've got to make a change for the better."

Chapter 3
Revelations of The Soul, Foolishness of The Heart

1

The bright morning light streamed through Tomeka's bedroom window and fell on her closed eyelids. Tomeka rolled onto her back and stared up at her twelve-foot ceiling. She thought about the extraordinary man she had met the night before.

"Amere Destiny…boy, you've got a name to live up to. If you are who I need you to be, I definitely won't be sleeping alone for much longer."

Tomeka looked at the clock on the wall. It was already ten-thirty. It was time to get her Saturday started.

"I better enjoy my day before the diva comes back."

The following afternoon, she would have to drive to Jonesboro to pick up her daughter, Janicia, from her mother's house. She picked up the cordless phone and called her mother to confirm the appointment. After the second ring, Tomeka's mother, Natalie, answered the phone.

"Hello?"

"Good morning, mom."

"How's my pumpkin?"

"Mom, I am too old to be called pumpkin!"

"You are never too old, pumpkin. You know the saying: The

older the wine, the more I can call you by your nickname."

"I see you are still messing up old sayings!"

"All-time leader!"

"What are you all doing?"

"Janicia and I just came in from the grocery store. We bought some ice cream and cones for later."

"Has Janicia been bad?"

"Bad is not the word. How about worst?" Natalie giggled.

"What?"

"I have had to constantly threaten to get a switch from the backyard to get her to act straight."

"Not my daughter!"

"Yes, part of your X and Y chromosomes!"

"I don't know what you are talking about," Tomeka laughed.

"What time are you coming to rescue me?" Natalie asked.

"What time are you going to church?"

"At eleven o'clock. When are you going to church?"

"Tomorrow. Right on the sofa. I think Jasper Williams, Creflo Dollar, and Joel Olsteen are playing back to back."

"Going to church on your couch doesn't count, Tomeka. When you go to your place of worship, you strengthen your belief in God."

"I know. I know."

"You don't know, Tomeka. When you don't go to worship, you lose out on your blessings."

"I am going to change that soon. I promise."

"Well, don't put today off for tomorrow. You can start by joining us at the eleven o'clock service tomorrow and bring your friend. What's his name? Tony, Jack..."

"It's Antone, Natalie, and we are not friends anymore!"

"When did this happen?" Natalie asked.

"Yesterday. That huge dinner I prepared was all for nothing!"

"When you cook for a man and he does not show up, something's wrong," Natalie advised.

"He didn't want to be in a relationship, mom."

"Oh, well, you did right. Antone needs to get right."

"There is no right for Antone. Something is going to have to happen to him before he makes a change."

"At least you don't have to worry about that baby's momma drama at all times of night."

"That's a relief."

"I told you a long time ago to let go. That's what's wrong with you young people these days—you don't know when to let go!"

"You're right. It would have been easier back then."

"I told you a long time ago; a soft head makes a what, pumpkin?"

"A soft—"

Natalie interrupted.

"Don't be cussing. You are not that grown!"

Tomeka laughed. She loved her mother and her unique teachings. With the unexpected death of her father, it was only natural that their relationship would grow in a more positive direction.

"Nat, I met someone last night."

"Whoa! You just broke up with Antone!"

"I know, but I can't let a man keep me down. You taught me that!"

"That's my girl! Nothing short of a diva!"

"Mom, he made me feel so comfortable."

"Sounds like a gentleman!"

"Correction. The perfect gentleman!"

"Give me the 411 'cause this does not sound like a rebounding fling," Natalie said.

"I will tell you how we met tomorrow after church."

"Ooh! I can't believe my little angel has met the perfect gentleman!"

"Calm down, mom. You're a little premature. He could be a nut case."

"But ahhh...he could be the real deal!"

"You're right, he could be...Mom, I know what you are trying to do."

"Huh?"

"You are trying to get me to talk about him, but I really called to speak to you. Now that we are done, can I speak to Janicia?"

"Janicia, your mother is on the phone!" Natalie yelled.

Tomeka could hear the patter of her daughter's feet on her mother's hardwood floor. Tomeka called Janicia by her nickname, Neesey.

"Hey, Nessey!"

"Hey, momma! Whatcha doing?" Janicia asked.

"Nothing. Just about to go visit some friends."

"Are they okay?"

Yes, Neesey. Have you been giving grandma any problems?"

"Uh uh! I have been a good girl."

"That's good 'cause if you've bad I am going to bring a switch home."

"No switch, momma!"

Tomeka laughed.

"Do you miss me, Neesey?"

"I miss you, momma."

"I miss you, too. I will be down there to pick you up tomorrow, okay?"

"Okay."

"I love you."

"I love you, too."

"Put grandma back on the phone."

"Okay! Grandma, the telephone!"

"You got my money?" Natalie asked in a deep voice.

"What money?"

"That money I let you borrow when you were ten," Natalie laughed.

"Mom, I am not studying you! I have to get up and get my day started."

"Make sure you wrap up when you go outside. The real Atlanta hawk is out!"

"Okay. I will be at church tomorrow. I love you, mom!"

"I love you, too, Pumpkin."

The loving mother and daughter ended their morning phone call. Tomeka hopped out of her bed. She strolled to her kitchen to make a mocha latté. Today, she would make a couple of surprise visits. First, Shelby; then, Peyton. She sat on her couch and thought about what her mother had said about missing her blessings. She decided to pray.

"Lord, I don't ask for much, but please give me a sign about this man I met last night. He seemed so right for me. Please give me a sign. Amen."

She continued to sit on her couch and sip her latte. On the other side of town, someone was thinking of her as well.

2

In the southern suburb city of Fayetteville, Amere Destiny was thinking of Tomeka. He was lying on his back dressed in a pair of boxer briefs. On his left knee, there was a wavy scar.

"Tomeka. Tomeka. Tomeka. I hope you are not the average shovel-packing woman who goes to the club. Lord, I would give up all these materialistic things if you would just send me a companion."

His washboard abs flexed slightly. He remembered the advice his coach had given him after he had broken his femur. Someone had undercut him while going up for a dunk. As a result, he had lost his contract with the Atlanta Fire Cats, the professional basketball team of the city, and his fiancée had walked out on him.

"Amere, everything, everything happens for a reason," his coach said. "You will get better and a woman will come into your life who appreciates you as a person and not for the digits in your bank account."

Five years had passed since that fateful event and Amere had constantly been dodging women until the previous day. Now, he had his heart set on one lady. He had one goal—to make Tomeka his.

"Ah! Tomeka, I could lay here and think of you all day, but it is time for my second job."

Every Saturday, Amere gave back to his local community, BONANZA, in Jonesboro at the outside basketball courts. In an hour, there would be thirteen twelve-year-old boys and one twelve-year-old girl waiting for him to assist in the development of their basketball skills and sportsmanship. These children were the closest thing he had to a family and he would not keep them waiting, not even for thoughts of Tomeka.

3

The dim morning sun streamed through a bay window in the kitchen. Shelby sat on a stool and slowly sipped a cup of hot chocolate. She had not slept a wink and the cold temperatures had crept into her home because she did not have the willpower to close the front door.

"He doesn't want me...he doesn't want the twins," Shelby said. Her tears mixed with her warm beverage.

"Why! Lord, why has this happened to me!? Why did I get betrayed? I wasn't in the streets lusting over other men? I was at home with my family? Why?"

She threw the cup of hot chocolate across the kitchen. It smashed into a cabinet filled with expensive china. Shelby walked into the living room, picked up a small African figurine, and threw it at the television in the theater room. Her frenzy did not cease. Shelby grabbed all the family pictures and tossed them into the fireplace.

"Damn this house, these pictures, and this life!"

Suddenly, the telephone rang. The unexpected sound snapped her from her path of destruction. She stood as still as an animal in the woods that had just detected a hunter. The phone rang again. Then, the answering machine clicked on. The message that she had recorded two years ago echoed throughout the house.

"Thank you for calling the Harrington residence! We are sorry we missed your phone call. Please leave your name and number at the beep and we will return your call promptly."

Following the beep, Benjamin shouted out in an angry voice, "Shelby, answer the phone. I know you are there! I am calling to let you in on a little secret."

Shelby slowly walked back into the kitchen as she heard Benjamin moaning. Shelby knew that sound. It was the sound that

Benjamin made while making love.

"Right there, baby. Ooh, yeah…"

"You bastard," Shelby whispered.

"Not so hard! Right there…ohhh! "Ah, that ice feels good, baby! You wouldn't have to do this if Shelby hadn't given me a hairline fracture on my ribs!"

Shelby bit her bottom lip until blood trickled forth and let out a deep breath as she realized that Benjamin wasn't having sex.

Finally, Benjamin finished his business and returned to his message.

"Of course, your lawyer will figure it out, but this will save you a consultation fee. Do you remember all of those business deals I was supposed to be attending month after month? Well, those business deals were all about me closing all my shops! You got it, sister. You're broke! Every fitness center I ever owned has been sold to an unknown buyer and I have liquidated all of my assets to an offshore account! 'I'm rich, bii—"

The answering machine cut Benjamin off, but the damage had been done. In a blind fury, Shelby ripped the answering machine from the wall and threw it to the floor. The machine repeatedly played the portion of the message concerning Benjamin selling all of his fitness centers and liquidating his assets.

"Well, those business deals were all about me closing shop, all my shops! Yep! You got it, sister. You're broke! Well, those business deals were all about me closing all my shops! Yep! You got it, sister. You're broke! "

"Whyyyyyy, Lord, Whyyyyy!" Shelby screamed.

She dropped to her knees as tears poured. Suddenly, her cell phone rang. She stumbled to her feet in a teary daze and found the cell phone beside a broken lamp. She glanced at the phone. The caller was her best friend through thick and thin, Tomeka.

"I need you, girl, but I can't talk about it right now. I just can't."

Shelby elected not to answer the phone. She stared as her phone display showed a pending voice mail. Shelby walked back to the kitchen. Benjamin's message had sent her into the deepest pit of depression.

"Well, those business deals were all about me closing shop, all my shops! Yep! You got it, sister. You're broke! Well, those business deals were all about me closing shop, all my shops! Yep! You got it, sister. You're broke!"

Shelby knew that Benjamin was diabolical and only announced his intentions when there was no margin for error. She knew this because when they met he was engaged to another woman.

"It's over! I have no money and I can't take care of my kids! I need to go to sleep."

Shelby walked upstairs and went into the twins' bathroom. She opened the medicine cabinet and reached far in the back. When she pulled her hand back, she held a bottle of sleeping pills. She drew herself a warm bath and began to sing her favorite childhood nursery rhyme.

"Rock-a-bye baby in the tree top!"

Shelby untwisted the top of the sleeping pills.

"When the wind blows, the cradle will rock!"

She turned the water low but not off.

"When the bough breaks, the cradle will fall!"

Shelby lowered her body into the tub until the warm water swirled around her neck.

"Down will come baby, cradle, and all! God have mercy on

me!"

Shelby turned up the bottle of pills to her mouth and swallowed. She dropped the bottle of pills onto the bathroom floor and waited for sleep to overtake her. Downstairs, the front door remained open.

4

Tomeka, dressed in a thick gray sweatsuit and her hair in a bouncy ponytail, exited her condo. As she stepped out of the elevator, the security guard addressed her.

"I kept the building safe for you last night. Did you have fun?"

"I had a fabulous time!"

"Good. I am off tomorrow, so I don't know who is going to protect your home."

"The same "who" that always has, the good Lord! Have a good day," Tomeka replied.

The security guard shook his head as Tomeka left the building.

"What is the world coming to? Go to the club one night, talk about the Lord the next morning?"

Tomeka maneuvered her truck out of the parking deck and turned her heater on HOT as she read the dashboard temperature display.

"Forty degrees! Yesterday, it was 68! The weatherman earned his paycheck today! Next stop, Shelby's house."

Tomeka drove for a short while and came to a red light. To her left, there was a strip of retail stores. People walked to and fro.

"I should stop at the jewelry store."

The light turned green and a few drivers behind her honked their car horns.

"Alright! I am moving!'

Tomeka sped into the northbound lane. For some reason, her need to see Shelby was urgent. Tomeka called Shelby's phone again but received the same result. Tomeka decided to leave her a message.

"Shelby, I know you are at home working out or getting dressed to go out! It's one of the two. You missed it last night, girl! I am back on the scene and on my way to tell you the whole story!"

Tomeka pressed the gas. In five minutes, she reached the luxury hillside community of Timber Hill. Several prominent people resided in this community. Tomeka crested a small hill. On the right, a lake and golf course stretched out before her. She made a left onto Shelby's street. As she coasted toward the cul-de-sac, Tomeka saw the front door was wide open! Someone had invaded Shelby's home!

"Shelby's in trouble! Lord, please let her be okay!"

Tomeka brought the car to a screeching halt in the driveway. She reached into the glove compartment where she kept her unloaded nine-millimeter handgun, Nina. Tomeka had purchased the gun after one of Byron's flings had threatened to beat her down. She loaded the handgun and put one in the chamber.

"They picked the wrong girl to mess with, Nina."

She ran into the house with her gun extended like a cop. The cold air had blown dry autumn leaves into the foyer. Tomeka stared at the broken items in the home.

Did a hurricane hit the room? What is going on?

Tomeka stepped around the broken glass and pottery. She was careful not to alert the intruder. She could hear a voice speaking, but the words were unclear.

"Mmm…"

Tomeka crept toward the sound. The voice was coming from the kitchen.

"Mmm..."

As she got closer, the voice became clearer. The voice belonged to Benjamin. Tomeka leapt into the kitchen with the gun extended in front of her.

"What did you do to my friend, you bastard?"

There was no one in the kitchen. Tomeka glanced around. It was the shattered answering machine that was repeating itself over and over.

"Well, those business deals were all about me closing all my shops! You got it, sister. You're broke!"

"Benjamin, how could you? Why would you?"

Tomeka ejected the tape and placed it in the pocket of her pants. Tomeka knew that she had to find Shelby. Tomeka left the kitchen and crept to the base of the stairs. She heard water running.

"Oh, my God!"

Tomeka sprinted up the steps. Halfway up, her sneakers squeaked. Water was on the steps.

"My God! The bath tub! Please, don't be drowned in the bathtub!"

Tomeka rounded the corner. Shelby was in the bathtub. She was unconscious. Her right arm rested limply on the edge of the tub. Suddenly, Shelby's head sank under the water.

"Shelby!"

Tomeka clicked the safety on her pistol to avoid a misfire as she dashed into toward her friend. Tomeka entered the bathroom and placed the pistol in the pouch of her sweatshirt. She grabbed Shelby by the collar of her thermal sweatsuit and hoisted her from under the water.

"Shelby! Shelby, wake up!"

Tomeka rapidly patted Shelby's face. Shelby's mouth opened. White foam oozed out. Tomeka wiped Shelby's mouth, turned off the water, and unplugged the tub.

"Shelby! Shelby! It's me, Tomeka! What did you do?"

Tomeka tugged at Shelby. Tomeka tried to gain leverage, but her foot slipped. She banged her knee on the side of the tub.

"What in the hell?"

Tomeka stooped down and picked up an empty white bottle. The labeling read Sleep Aid, 100 tablets.

"100 tablets!"

The possibility of Shelby having taken at least one hundred sleeping pills gave Tomeka unbelievable strength. She grabbed Shelby and heaved her from the tub with tremendous force.

"Aggggh!"

Tomeka sat on the floor with Shelby's head in her lap. Tomeka flipped out her cell phone and called 911.

"Come on! Connect stupid cell phone!"

Finally, the phone call connected. A friendly feminine voice greeted Tomeka on the other end.

"911. This is Operator Twenty-Five. How may I help you?"

"My friend has overdosed on sleeping pills!"

"Ma'am, please calm down."

"She could have taken all one hundred for all I know! Hurry! Please!"

"Ma'am, I need you to calm down. What is your name?"

"My name is Tomeka."

"What is the address of the complaint?"

"I am at 1589 Timber Trail Dunwoody in the Timber Hill golf community! Hurry, she is unconscious! Please, God! Hurry!"

There was a rapid sound of keystrokes as Operator Twenty-Five put extensive emergency training to use. She quickly processed the information and dispatched a unit.

"EMS is en route to your location, Tomeka."

"You're the best!"

"Thank you. Tomeka, I need you to calm down and talk to me."

"Okay."

"Tell me about your friend. Is she breathing?"

"No. Oh, God! No!"

"Tomeka, calm down and take a deep breath."

"O-okay."

"Look around the room and find a hand mirror. She could be breathing very softy. Place the mirror in front of her face and tell me what happens."

Tomeka followed the commands and located a hand mirror on the nearby sink. She placed it close to Shelby's face. A thin fog appeared.

"She is breathing! She is breathing!"

"Excellent! Is the pulse fast or slow?"

"How do I check that?"

"Use the pads of your fingers, not your fingertips, or thumbs and place them on the right side of your friend's neck. Can you check that for me?"

"Yes, I-I can do that."

"You are doing great, Tomeka."

Not too far away, Tomeka heard the sound of sirens blaring.

"Is it fast or slow?"

"It is very slow."

"God have mercy," Operator Twenty-five said.

Suddenly, the sirens grew louder and filled the cul-de-sac. The paramedics had arrived!

"Operator, the paramedics are here! Thank you for helping me! I have to go!"

"You are welcome! I will be praying for her recovery," Operator Twenty-Five responded.

The call ended.

"Up here! Up here!"

The medical personnel heard Tomeka's cries and rushed up the stairs. Two paramedics entered the bathroom with a gurney.

"Dispatch, we are on the scene and securing the patient," one of the uniformed men reported.

They quickly hoisted Shelby onto the gurney and carried her down the stairs.

"Ma'am, are you riding in the back with the patient?"

"Yes, but I need my purse."

"Hurry!"

Tomeka sprinted to her truck and put her gun back into the glove department. Then, she grabbed her purse and leapt into the back of the ambulance. She held Shelby's hand and prayed.

"Father God, please...please, don't take my friend. She has a family that needs her. Please!"

The ambulance sped toward Northern Regional Hospital. Tomeka remembered the tape that she ejected from the answering machine and knew Benjamin was responsible.

"Once you get stable, Shelby, I am going to get to the bottom of this. Benjamin is going to pay!"

5

Amere blew the whistle at the signal of Lamar's time-out request.

"Time-out. Blue team," Amere said.

He took the basketball and set it down at mid-court. The blue and black teams retreated to their respective benches. All but one jersey had the word KING across the front of the uniform. The only girl on the team had the word QUEEN on hers. Now, Amere watched how the two teams handled adversity. What he saw wasn't pretty.

"They pushin' me!" Scottie of the black team yelled.

"You need to pass the ball!" Red yelled.

"What are you doing? Why are you walking the ball up?" Tisha of the blue team complained.

"I'm playing harder than you," Lamar yelled.

"You're too slow to ever play harder than me!"

Amere shook his head and assumed his dual role as coach of the blue team and the black team. It was during times like this he was glad that he had decided to give back. Amere approached the black team first.

"Quante, Red, Mike, Steven, Vince, Keno, and Scottie, what type of defense are ya'll playing?" Amere asked.

"Umm—," Mike began.

"Slim and none. You all are not playing. You are fussing with each other!" Amere interjected.

"They pushing out there, Amere!" Scottie said.

"People push in real life, Scottie. So, does that mean you are gonna complain when it happens?"

"No."

"So, why complain now? The adversity that you face on this

court will be the same adversity you face in the real world!" Amere coached.

"How do we turn things around?" Quante asked.

"Yeah, Amere. How do we do that?" Keno asked.

Amere looked at the seven thirteen-year-old kids. He owed them a truthful answer that would help them out in areas beyond basketball. Amere relayed his message via the acronym T.E.A.M.

"You perform as a team. Do you know what T.E.A.M stands for?"

"It means working together," Red answered.

"That's right! Even more, T.E.A.M. stands for Together Each Achieves More!"

"That's what I'm talking bout," Vince said.

"Now, everyone put your hands on my hand and yell 'TEAM'. We are one team trying to accomplish one common goal!"

The kids nodded their heads. Amere took his fist and punched his palm.

"You are better than those thirty five points on the scoreboard! When you work as a team you never loose! Put your hands in!"

Amere stretched out his hand and the seven guys stick out theirs.

"Do you feel that? What you feel is team. Now, let me hear you say it on three. One...two... three..."

"TEAM!"

Amere left the newly inspired group. With every meeting, he tried to instill the concepts of hard work and integrity in the kids. Now, Amere trotted over to the blue team.

"Tisha, why were you yelling at Lamar?" Amere asked.

"Because he wants to walk the ball up the court!"

"And what would you like for him to do?"

"I wanna run!"

Amere glanced over at the scoreboard.

"How many points are you ahead, Tisha?" Amere asked.

"Two."

"Two too less. When your lead disappears, so does your team."

"You trippin', Amere," Marcel quipped.

"Marcel, what's your problem?" Amere asked.

"Tisha keeps pointing her finger at everyone, but she threw the ball away two times!"

"So, what about you, Tony?" Amere asked as he turned to Tony.

"Ain't no one moving. We just standing there. Tisha won't call a play," he replied.

"A leader doesn't do the things that you just did, Tisha. A leader listens to those around her, motivates them, and influences them to complete the job at hand."

"And what does that have to do with me?"

"No one wants to play with you! They don't want to play because of you!"

Tisha dropped her head as she realized the truth.

"Pick your head up, Tisha. You are the point-guard, the leader of the pack. Listen to your team, formulate a plan, and work that plan! Can you do that?"

"Yeah. Team, I am sorry for snapping. Let's do it!"

"On the count of three, let me hear you say 'Work that plan!' One... two... three..."

"WORK THAT PLAN!"

Amere trotted to the middle of the basketball court and picked up the basketball. As he trotted to the sideline, Amere dribbled behind his back, did figure-eights through his legs, and twirled the ball on his index finger.

"Who are we?" Antone yelled.

Both teams answered at the same time.

"KINGS AND A QUEEN!"

"Blue ball on the sideline. Two minutes left. Thirty five- thirty-seven! Play as a team! Work that plan!"

Amere blew his whistle and Lamar took the ball out of bounds. Tisha brought the ball up and called a play.

"Detroit left!" she yelled.

Marcel turned and set a screen for Tony. Tony faked right and went left. Tisha passed him the ball. Tony jumped up to shoot, but Scottie jumped up to block the shot. Tony adjusted and passed the ball to Lamar. Lamar leapt in the air and slapped the backboard for a lay up.

"Ugh! Good pass, Tony!" Lamar yelled.

Steven brought the ball down the court and called for a clear out. He crossed his opponent over and dribbled towards the hoop. He leapt into the air and so did Marcel. Steven read the move and passed the ball behind his back to Red. Red caught the ball and quickly passed it to Quante, who shot a three-pointer.

"Swish!" the nets said.

Before the ball could bounce, Scottie was calling for pressure.

"Summertime! Summertime!"

The pressure was on as two guards got up on the ball. Another person dropped to the middle, and two people dropped back. Amere sat back and let the clock run out as the kids became lost in the competitive game. His only wish was that Tomeka was there.

"Tomeka, why haven't you called?" Amere whispered.

While Amere watched the basketball game, at Northern Regional

Hospital, Shelby was trying to win a second chance at the game of life.

6

In a hospital room, Shelby rested. Tomeka sat beside Shelby. She had just finished talking to Shelby's mom. She and Shelby's sisters would be arriving soon.

"Amere, I want to call you, but I can't," Tomeka said.

She held Shelby's hand. The painkillers that were administered to Shelby were doing their job by keeping her sedated. When she first arrived, the nurses had to strap Shelby down to put a tube her throat.

"Lord, h-how did it get to this?"

Tomeka quietly wept as a machine quietly pumped a yellowish fluid from a plastic bag and into Shelby's arm. At that moment, the on-call physician visited Shelby's room. He had a slim build and was dressed in a white lab coat with a rainbow pin attached to the collar of the coat. His straight black hair was parted on the right side. The tone of his voice was high pitched with a Middle Eastern accent.

"Ello. Is dis Shelby Harrington?"

"Yes, it is," Tomeka said.

"Are you, Tomeka?"

"Yes. What is that information on the chart?"

"Dis information pertains to Shelby's allergies, etc."

"Doctor, may I ask your name?"

"I am sorry for being, how do you say, rude. My name is Dr. Crabi."

"Nice to meet you," Tomeka said.

As Tomeka wiped her teary eyes, Dr. Crabi reached into his

jacket pocket and extracted a small pack of scented tissue.

"Thank you. Today has been tough."

"Keep them. The powdery scent of the tissue makes light of tough moments."

"That is so sweet of you."

"Well, thank you. I hate to see any person as beautiful as your friend go through such a terrible ding."

Tomeka dried her tears and tossed the wad of tissue into a nearby trashcan.

"It is such a terrible thing," Tomeka said.

"Do you know what could have pushed her to such an extremely drastic measure? Does she have a history of depression or drug abuse?"

"Shelby is not a junkie! Those pills were prescribed to her last year when she had developed a mild case of insomnia!"

"Tomeka, please understand. I am not passing judgment on your friend. I am simply trying to discover her behavior."

"Sorry. I am a little defensive. Shelby has always been high-spirited, always working out, and very fond of living! This is not like her!"

"Okay. What caused you to visit her this morning?"

"I don't know. I just had this feeling, you know. Have you ever felt like you just had to do something?"

"I can relate to the sensation."

"Well, when I woke up this morning, I had this urge to go see Shelby. I could not ignore it. I am just blessed that I got there in time."

"Five minutes later and your friend would have died."

"Then, it was meant for me to save her."

"Your friend swallowed enough pills to put a village to sleep. I have seen cancer stage three reverse to nothing. Your story is just as significant."

"It was nothing."

"But it was something. Because of you, she will live to see another day!"

"Do you know when Shelby will be released?"

"Whenever a person has a chronic history of depression or overdoses on drugs, it is procedure to admit that person to an extensive psychiatric evaluation."

"You don't want to release her and she kills herself," Tomeka said.

"There could be some legal ramifications for such rash action."

"What if I had evidence proving that something other than drugs caused her to do this to herself?"

Dr. Crabi raised an eyebrow.

"And what type of evidence would that be?"

Tomeka stood up. Dr. Crabi noticed the curve of Tomeka's hips as she reached into her pocket and extracted a tape.

"When I made it to my friend's house, a portion of a message was playing on her broken answering machine. I think this is the clue we need to know why Shelby did what she did."

"Yes, please follow me to my office."

Tomeka and Dr. Crabi exited Shelby's room and silently walked down the corridor that led to his office. As they walked, Tomeka noticed the patients that were resting in the rooms.

"There are so many of them. Are these rooms ever empty?"

"Only when they pass to the other side," Dr. Crabi responded.

"Hospitals are places where people go to die. I never want to be hooked up to a machine."

"Not even if it would help determine whether or not you live?"

"I don't want to suffer. If a machine is breathing for me, then I am not supposed to be here. It's time for me to go meet the King!"

"You Americans, so proud."

They entered Dr. Crabi's spacious office. Tomeka noticed the various certificates, medals, and awards of recognition within a glass cabinet.

"You were the youngest in your graduating class?" Tomeka asked.

"Yes. I was fourteen."

"How did you deal with the pressure?"

"Hmm. I looked at it like this—pressure takes coal and forms diamonds!"

"I see that you are an art collector, also" Tomeka said.

"Yes, abstract. I like the colors and the questions that they cause to arise. Is it a nose, a bus, or a bird?"

"Or a leprechaun?"

The two laughed.

"I picked out the purple drapes and valances on the windows."

"Nice touch. When I sit in your office, I can tell that you care," Tomeka complimented

"Thank you. Now, for your tape."

Dr. Crabi removed his cassette tape and inserted Tomeka's tape. There was a mechanical noise as Dr. Crabi rewound the tape. He pressed play. They listened as the message played.

"Shelby, answer the phone! I know you are there! I am calling to let you in on a little secret. Right there, baby. Ooh, yeah...not so hard! Right there...ohhh. Ah, that ice feels good, baby! You

wouldn't have to do this if Shelby hadn't given me a hairline fracture on my ribs!"

Tomeka pressed the pause button.

"Is someone kissing in the background?" Dr Crabi asked.

"I don't know, but that's Benjamin's voice. If Shelby kicked him, then he did something to deserve it."

Tomeka pressed play and they continued to listen.

"Of course, your lawyer will figure it out, but at least this will save you a consultation fee. Do you remember all of those business deals I was attending month after month?"

Tomeka drew close. This was the moment of truth.

Well, those business deals were all about me closing all shops! You got it, sister. You're broke!

Tomeka paused the tape.

"The cat's out of the bag. I can't believe Benjamin is acting like this!"

"I must agree. The message is most disturbing. We don't have to continue."

"Yes, we do."

Tomeka pressed play.

"Every fitness center I ever owned has been sold to an unknown buyer and I have liquidated all of my assets to an off shore account! I'm rich bii—"

The tape automatically stopped. Tomeka sat down. Her legs were weak.

"That bastard! No wonder she felt that she didn't have anything to live for! Lord, please, have mercy!"

"Curses to that Benjamin. He is a poor excuse for a man!"

Dr. Crabi ejected the tape and handed it to Tomeka.

"She is going to need a lawyer—a good lawyer."

"The tape will be a decisive ally in the court of law. In my country, we have a saying—the revelations of the soul and the foolishness of the heart will sometimes eliminate the best qualities of a person and reduce them to a fraction of their former self."

"So, what does that actually mean?"

Tomeka placed the tape in her purse.

"It means the truth is always true. Actions may deceive but the true nature of a person cannot remain hidden."

"I believe the great Maya Angelou said when people show you who they are, believe them," Tomeka paraphrased.

"That is exactly what I was trying to say! The want of love, affection, and companionship causes people to become different!"

Tomeka rationalized with Dr. Crabi. She could never have engaged in an in-depth conversation like this with Antone.

"Everyone wants to be loved. Some people want to be loved by any means necessary."

"Where I am from, the matters of the heart are very serious and are not to be toyed with. If a man is caught cheating, he is put to death by spider bite!"

"And where might that be?"

"Mars."

They both laughed. As the laughter died down, Dr. Crabi continued the conversation.

"I will tell you only if you will accompany me to the cafeteria for lunch? I would like to learn more of your thought process."

"I am a little hungry. Perhaps a muffin will do me."

Tomeka and Dr. Crabi left the office. Tomeka kept both eyes opened. Dr. Crabi seemed to have other motives for his actions.

7

Peyton observed Juan as he fought for his life in the intensive care unit of Northern Regional Hospital. Peyton was dressed in a blue long sleeve Northern Regional T-shirt and blue sweats donated by the hospital. Doctor Hamilton stood before Peyton with a clipboard. A kind nurse had taken Itty Bitty to the nursery where she could play with other children while Peyton discussed her husband's status.

"Mrs. Suarez, you must prepare yourself for the worst," Dr. Hamilton said.

"How much damage has been done?" Peyton asked.

"The bullet traveled through your husband's lower abdominal area. It shattered his liver and spleen."

"Oh, my God."

"The bullet caused massive hemorrhaging in the lower cavity."

"Ahh."

"We had to move quickly and replace his liver. If his body rejects the organ, his 50/50 survival rate diminishes. I am so sorry."

"Oh, God!" Peyton wept. The tears stung her eyes.

"I would suggest you pray. I will now leave you alone."

Seconds after Doctor Hamilton left the room, she ceased her crying and stared at Juan lying unconscious with an oxygen tube taped to his nose.

"How did you find out about me and Byron? Did you find my love mails?"

"I'm sorry, Juan, but Byron is a better lover with more money," Peyton confessed. "I've seen your life insurance policy. I could unplug this oxygen tube and walk out the room. Then, I would be free! I could send Itty Bitty to a nanny and be a football player's wife."

Peyton fiddled with the tubes of oxygen as she contemplated pulling the plug.

"I am a lot of things, Juan, but murder is not part of my profile. The doctor said that I should pray."

Peyton scoffed.

"I will pray that Tomeka doesn't find out about me and Byron."

Peyton stooped over Juan and whispered in his ear.

"I don't want you to make it!"

Peyton got up and looked in the mirror. Her eyes were bruised so bad that it hurt to blink, let alone cry.

"Luckily, my hair is long enough to cover up these bruises."

As Peyton styled her hair in the mirror, her guilty conscious spoke. *Tomeka is going to do more than bruise you...*

"Tomeka will not find out! Leave me alone!"

As an abused woman, Peyton had developed a conscious that spoke to her and guided her. The conscious was so real that it was the equivalent of another person.

Juan is going to live...

"That remains to be seen. If I want to, I can pull the plug!"

Tomeka even told you she was thinking of getting back with Byron...

"You heifer!"

Peyton spit into the mirror. Her stomach growled and she realized she had not had anything to eat since yesterday at the mall. On cue, the on-call nurse waltzed into the room silently reading from the chart she held in her hand.

"Oooh! Suga honey, that sounds like a prehistoric monster! RRRAAHH!"

Peyton looked at the nurse and struggled not to curse her out.

"When was the last time you had something to eat? Was it at the Last Supper?"

"Umm. And your name is?"

"Right her above the pocket, suga honey. I'm Nurse Ann."

"Pleased to meet you."

Peyton reached out to shake her hand, but Nurse Ann shook her head.

"Too many germs, suga honey. Staph is a stalker; it's hard to get rid of!"

Peyton giggled at Nurse Ann's attitude. The nurse's attitude reminded her of her two best friends.

Best friends don't sleep with each others' babies' fathers...

Peyton blocked out her guilty conscious and responded to the nurse.

"Yeah, it's been a while since I had something to eat. Does the cafeteria have good food?"

"Ummm-hmmm! They have the best turkey and dressing on the north side of town, suga honey! Haven't you ever heard of the A.Y.C.E.S?"

Peyton scratched her head.

"No, I have not heard of aseize. I don't come to hospitals that often."

"No, A.Y.C.E.S like aces in a card deck, suga honey. Well, anyway, it is the "All You Can Eat and Some" for only two-fifty. Yep, two-fifty!"

"Two dollars and fifty cents?"

"Well, it started at noon, so if we get movin' we can beat that long line. I am due for a break."

"But—"

"Is that your hubby, suga honey?"

"Yes."

"Honey suga, you won't do him any good if we have to admit you to another room for malnourishment!"

Nurse Ann recorded the numbers on the machine that displayed Juan's blood pressure and heart rate.

"I need to be here to watch him. Something could happen."

"Yeah, you could fall out from hunger! He is in the hospital bed. Let's keep you out one!"

"Thanks," Peyton responded.

"Seriously, suga, don't worry about leaving your husband. The medication will not wear off for another hour or so. You will still be the first person he sees when he wakes up."

"Are you sure?"

Nurse Ann raised her left arm and took a sniff.

"Yes, I am sure."

"Ha! Ha!"

"Listen, honey suga, women like you and I have to stick together. We are good women. Do you understand where I am coming from?"

"Yeah…I guess so."

"Since God made this green earth with blue skies, there have been women like you and me."

"And what type of lady is that?"

"A lady who loves her other half to the fullest."

Peyton let an uneasy giggle escape from her mouth as Nurse Ann touched her on the shoulder.

"You have a handsome king. When he wakes, he is going to want to see his beautiful queen."

Peyton touched her bruised face.

"Thanks. I hope that is what he will see."

"Even though you are bruised up, you are still beautiful. Honey suga, you are making me want to see my slender light-skinned kin! What time is it?"

"It's almost one o'clock."

"Let's go. My other half should be in the cafeteria at this time."

"Okay. Let's go."

Peyton put on a pair of black sunglasses and followed Nurse Ann to the end of the well-lit hallway and into an elevator.

"You watch what I say, honey suga. You are going to eat like you are at a casino in New Orleans!"

"I only wish."

Without any further stops, the elevator descended to the ground floor. The doors opened and the aroma of soul food drifted in. Peyton reached in her pocket and pulled out the five dollars that the paramedics had donated to her. Today, she would eat like a queen.

8

Tomeka made herself swallow a portion of her Salisbury steak. The meat was not seasoned correctly and reminded her of a fat-free soybean burger that only Shelby would be interested in.

"The steak needs some season. I should have gotten the turkey and dressing," Tomeka said.

"Salt is bad for you. It causes hypertension," Dr.Crabi replied.

Dr. Crabi cut a slice of his Salisbury steak. Tomeka winced at how the doctor easily ate the bland meat. She knew she shouldn't have listened to him and, instead, should have chosen her own food.

"I am sorry, but I can't eat it. It's too…what's the word…oh yeah, healthy. Yeah, it's too healthy!"

"That is because of the mad cow scare that they use soy instead of real beef."   "Then you have mine."

Tomeka closed her carry-out container and pushed it to the side. She took a good look at Dr. Crabi as her womanly intuition clocked in for work.

"Doctor?"

"Yes."

"We have been sitting in here for more than thirty minutes and you have not asked me anything about my friend, her husband, or even myself."

"We were eating. In my country, it is rude to talk and eat."

"Well, Dr. Crabi, if you haven't noticed, this isn't your country. In this country, when a man goes to lunch with a lady, there is always some suggested conversation," Tomeka said.

"Suggested conversation? What is that?"

"That is when you tell me why we are at lunch."

"We are at lunch because we are hungry."

"Oh no, you don't! Don't play games with me, doctor. What are your intentions?"

Dr. Crabi wiped his mouth with the edge of his napkin. Tomeka's aggressive demeanor was more of a turn-on than her bedroom eyes. There was no fooling Tomeka. No need to beat around the bush.

"At first, I was captured by your beauty. In my country, only princes would be allowed to speak to you," Dr. Crabi said.

Tomeka blushed.

"I have that effect now."

"Only in America! I love black women. You are so aggressive!"

"Cut the aggressive crap. I do not lead people on. Tell me what is on your mind."

Dr. Crabi shifted in his seat and loosened his pink and white tie. He leaned back and crossed one leg over the other. The doctor addressed Tomeka in a confident voice that was void of his foreign accent.

"Tomeka, when I saw you crying for your friend, I wanted to make all of your pain go away."

"Thank you for the thought."

"You are so beautiful and I could give you whatever a woman wants or needs. You would never have to work again. I could get your nails done and—"

"What the fuck is this, honey suga!"

Tomeka's and Dr. Crabi's heads snapped to the right as an angry nurse walked toward them. Not too far behind, another lady followed who wore sunglasses.

"So, this is why you quit calling me? You quit calling me for this?"

"Doctor, it looks like you have a patient," Tomeka said.

Tomeka gathered her items.

"You have the audacity to bring your new broad to the cafeteria like I wasn't going to see you!"

Tomeka stood to her feet and looked the angry nurse in the eye.

"Look, don't make this misunderstanding become a misunderstanding," Tomeka said.

"Tomeka, this is Nurse Ann. She is an old girlfriend. W-we just broke up a little while ago."

"A little while ago? You quit calling me on Monday and today is Saturday!"

"I'm a little too grown for this. You all have a nice life!"

As Tomeka left the table, the girl who followed behind the nurse stared at her from across the room. One thing Tomeka hated was someone who was too scared to talk.

"What are you looking at?"

Trying to avoid a confrontation, the girl limped away. Nurse Ann was still fired up. She rolled her eyes at Tomeka and snapped her fingers.

"I see what type of party this is. She is cute, but she is not Nurse Ann! She's a little short, don't you think?"

"I can explain," Dr. Crabi said.

"Don't bother. Just remember, nurse, large ass whuppins come in small packages! I don't want your man!"

"Ha! Ha! Ha!"

"What's so funny?" Tomeka asked.

"Ohhh! Honey suga! You've been hoodwinked! This isn't my man! This is my woman!"

"You're a freaking woman! I don't lick carpet or bump cooch!" Tomeka yelled.

Tomeka's eyes widened as certain hidden feminine attributes leapt to her attention. She stared at the frail body and the rainbow pin. She remembered the valances and curtains in the office, the high-pitched voice, and the scented tissue.

"I was going to tell you," Dr. Crabi said in a quiet voice.

"You tried me! I can't believe you tried me!"

At that moment, someone called out her name.

"Tomeka!"

Tomeka looked around and saw the woman with the sunglasses waving at her.

"Tomeka, over here! It's Peyton!"

Tomeka was elated. She walked toward Peyton. Suddenly, she turned around and directed some choice words to Dr. Crabi.

"Doctor, I will be requesting another physician to watch over my friend before you try her, too, you imposter."

Having had her say, she left Nurse Ann to deal with Dr. Crabi and her deceitful ways.

9

As Tomeka neared her friend, she saw why Peyton was wearing the dark sunglasses. Her complexion was slightly bruised along her cheeks. Tomeka's heart pounded in her chest. She grasped Peyton's wrist.

"What happened to you? Were you in a car wreck?" Tomeka asked.

"Ouch!"

Peyton wrenched away from Tomeka's touch.

"I barely touched you! What's wrong?"

"Nothing is wrong!"

Tomeka stepped into Peyton's face and whispered in a voice low enough for only her to hear.

"I am going to ask you once. Who beat you?"

"I I-I can't?"

"Peyton, I need you to try. Who beat you?"

Tomeka watched as Peyton struggled to tell her the truth. She took several deep breaths. Tears dripped from under the shades. Finally, she spoke, but her voice cracked.

"J-Jack did it. J-Jack did it!"

Tomeka embraced her traumatized friend and cried with her. The few people in the cafeteria applauded. Nurse Ann nudged Dr. Crabi in the arm.

"Honey suga, why can't we hug like that? Can't you feel the

love?"

When Tomeka and Peyton separated, Peyton explained.

"J-Jack, h-he beat me and shot Juan yesterday! Th-that's why I didn't g-go with you last night!"

"Is Juan okay? I mean he isn't..."

"No, he isn't dead, but he has a 50/50 chance."

"I feel so shallow. I thought that you had stood me up!"

"I would never let you down," Petyon said.

"I won't ever let you down. Have you had anything to eat?"

"Y-Yes. Nurse Ann bought my food."

"That trick has some type of sense."

"I did not know she was gay until she saw her old girlfriend talking to you. She went from glad to mad!"

"Yeah! Well, I hope they make up. I am here with Shelby. She overdosed on sleeping pills this morning."

"What!" Peyton exclaimed.

"Thank God I made it to her before the worst could happen."

"What part of the hospital is she in?"

"She is recovering in the critical care unit."

"Will she be okay?"

"Yes. They pumped her stomach. I will tell you the story later, but first I want see Juan."

"Are you sure?"

"Yes, we are too close now to be apart!"

Peyton smiled. This was exactly what she needed during this bad time—a good friend. Hopefully, Juan would still be asleep. They entered the elevator and Tomeka told Peyton about the previous night.

"Girl, let me tell you about last night. Antone was at the club with another girl!"

"Just like that?"

"Just like that! He even dedicated a song to her!"

"Which song?"

"That song called "Slow Jamz". You know when Twista be rapping fast."

"Yeah, I know that one."

"I was in VIP trying to absorb all that was going on!"

"I know it was hard to see Antone with someone new so fast. I don't know if I could have taken that. You know seeing Juan with someone else!"

"It was so hard for me to keep my composure. It hurt more knowing that he was with someone than seeing him with someone."

The doors of the elevator opened and they made their way down the hall.

"To make a long story short, as I tried to leave the VIP room, Antone saw me and bumped into a group of girls and spilled their drinks."

"Spilled drinks always cause fights."

"Just like lying and cheating. Antone grabbed me by the arm and one of the girls punched him in face!"

Tomeka stopped her allegory as she caught a glimpse of the nurses at the nurse's station pointing and frowning at them.

"Why are the nurses whispering and looking at us like that?" Tomeka asked.

"Um, I don't know. Maybe we were talking too loud," Peyton said.

"I'll tell you the rest inside."

They stopped before a closed door with Juan Suarez written on a removable label. They opened the door and walked inside. The room was quiet and Juan was asleep.

"I can't bear to see him like this," Peyton cried.

"It will pass. It will pass, Peyton."

"I know but it hurts so much."

Tomeka walked to the edge of the bed. Life and love were so important. She had these two treasures in Shelby and Peyton. These two treasures could be here one day and gone the next.

"If you guys ever need anything, just let me know. I promise to never let you down."

"We appreciate it, Tomeka. You are good people."

"Tomeka, you are good people. Too bad Peyton can't say the same thing," Juan interjected.

Peyton jerked the sunglasses from her face and stepped backwards.

"It can't be! You're awake!"

"Yes, I am awake and I have been praying for this moment to come ever since you left with the nurse. Tomeka—"

Peyton interrupted.

"Tomeka, I am about to ring for the nurse. She said the medication would cause hallucinations!"

"Go ahead. I already told the nurses the same story that I am about to tell Tomeka, except, this time, I won't leave out any details."

"The nurses were just pointing at us," Tomeka said.

She noticed that Peyton was sweating profusely and had a panic-stricken look on her face. Something was wrong. Tomeka locked eyes with Juan as he laid on his bed of affliction. His eyes darted from right to left as he struggled to start.

"Juan, take your time. Tell me why the nurses were pointing at us," Tomeka said.

"Yesterday, I received a phone call and the caller hung up on me. The caller was Jack, Peyton's baby's crazy father."

"I follow you," Tomeka said.

"There was a second call right after Jack hung up on me. When I answered that time, a guy replied that he had the wrong number. I quickly wrote down the telephone number from the caller ID screen. It had an area code of 504."

Across the room, Peyton sat on the sofa and bit her fingernails.

"So, what does this have to do with me, Juan?"

"Ooooh," Peyton sniffled.

"Water...Tomeka, give me some water, so I can finish."

"Peyton—"

Juan interrupted Tomeka in a hoarse voice.

"No! No! I don't want anything from her! She threatened to unplug my oxygen!"

"Calm down. See, I have your water."

Tomeka lowered the cup so that the straw was level with Juan's dry lips.

Peyton's sniffling had become a noisy whimper.

"Peyton, girl, get a hold of yourself," Tomeka said.

Tomeka was about to come to her friend's aid when Juan grasped Tomeka by the forearm and held her in place.

"Don't do it! Just hear me out, Tomeka. Then, decide if you want to help her, talk to her, or be around her again! Please, take a seat!"

Tomeka pulled a nearby chair to the bed.

"Tomeka, when I called the number, a front desk clerk answered the phone at the Omni Royal of New Orleans and told me she could not trace the number because there were numerous rooms at the hotel."

"When Peyton went to the store, I searched the phone records that were online. This produced little or nothing. In an act of desperation, I hacked into her e-mail account and discovered a load of romantic e-mails to a person she had been seeing, making love with, and planning to have a child with. Before I could leave the house to see my divorce lawyer, Jack did this to me."

"Juan, I am sorry you and Peyton are having problems, but this, this has nothing to do with me," Tomeka said.

"Tomeka, Peyton does not have to work Sunday. Peyton was going to be on her way to the Omni Royal of New Orleans where she was going to spend a couple of days with Byron Smith! She's been fucking him since last summer!"

"Peyton, how could you?"

"I messed up, Tomeka! I messed up!"

"I trusted you! You know I still have feelings for Byron!"

"I messed up! I messed up!"

"You lying, sneaking, hood rat! After all that I have done for you, and after all we have been through, you are screwing with my baby's daddy!"

"I MESSED UP!"

"You were never my friend! I even told you I still cared for Byron and wanted to be a family! You bitch, I hate you!"

"Agggh!"

Peyton sprinted out the door and Tomeka broke down in tears. Every man she had ever given a chance had misused her.

"When will the madness stop? When will someone love me like

I love him?"

Tomeka thought of Amere. Is he God-fearing? At that moment, she could not make the determination, but his genuine chivalry and candor had won her over. There was still hope for her.

"Juan, do you have anyone who can be here with you? I have to go. I can't stay here."

"Yes. I had the nurse to call my family. They should be here any minute. I am so sorry but I had to tell you."

"No, don't be. I want to thank you and I hope everything works out for you."

"Gracias, mi amiga," Juan responded.

Tomeka slowly rose from her seat and headed to the door. After stopping by the nurses' station to be sure that Juan was left in good hands, Tomeka returned to Shelby's room. Shelby was still fast asleep, but her family was there. Tomeka hugged Shelby's sisters and mother.

"Hi! How are y'all?" Tomeka greeted.

"We are fine! Thank you for staying with Shelby and saving her life," Ruby said.

"No problem. That is what friends are for!"

"Well, you are not a friend. You are a sister," Latreese said.

"Thanks again. Before I go, I need to tell you all something."

"What's that?" Ruby asked.

"Shelby's doctor is a cross-dresser. Dr. Crabi is really a woman!"

"That's a bird that won't fly," Ruby replied as she shook her head.

"I just didn't want you to get tricked like I did."

"Don't worry. We will keep all our eyes on her," Charlene said.

"Okay, I will check in later."

As Tomeka left the room, Ruby stared at her daughter and contemplated.

10

Ruby sat with one hand on her Bible and her other hand holding Shelby's. She had already prayed and sobbed until her throat became sore. Latreese and the others had gone downstairs to get some food from the cafeteria. It was just her, Shelby, and the machines that were helping her body recuperate.

Beep...Beep!

"Shelby, I remember walking you to the bus stop when you were in kindergarten. I remember you waving good-bye out the bus window as you went around the corner," Ruby said.

Beep...Beep!

"Shelby, I remember every spelling bee, every basketball game, and track meet you ever competed in!"

Ruby laughed as she wiped her teary eyes. The memories were vivid. She sat there and rubbed her eyes with her thumb and first finger.

"I remember when that rough-looking girl with those big calf muscles said she was going to smoke you like a cigar—nice and slow!"

Ruby laughed aloud.

"Right before the announcer yelled 'Go,' she spit on your hand. That day you ran like the wind!"

Beep...Beep!

"That girl cried like a baby. I remember seeing you shake her hand with the one she spat on! I taught you so well!"

Ruby succumbed to the memories and broke out in a new burst of tears. She stared at Shelby silently lying there as the machines monitored her status.

"No man is worth your life, Shelby! No man! No matter who he is or how much money he makes!"

Ruby wiped her tears with her handkerchief. Then, she opened her Bible and read from the book of Matthew.

"Shelby, the good book says, 'Thou shall love the Lord thy God with all thy heart, and with all thy soul, and with all thy mind.'"

Beep...Beep!

"'The second is like unto it, thou shall love thy neighbor as thyself.' Shelby, when you get better, I want you to forgive him!"

Beep...Beep!

"Forgiveness is the first step of healing."

Beep...Beep!

"Benjamin hasn't taken anything from you that the Lord hasn't already given you! God made you, not Benjamin! God has brought you to this and He will bring you through, feet first!"

Ruby laid her head on Shelby's hand. Her daughter's hand was cold.

"Please, Lord, let my Shelby wake up! Please!"

Tears dripped from her eyes and onto Shelby's hand. Suddenly, Ruby felt Shelby's hand becoming warmer. The hand twitched and the beeps of the monitor became steady.

Beep. Beep. Beep!

Ruby looked up as Shelby opened her eyes.

"Shelby, you're awake! Thank you, Lord! Thank you, Lord!"

Shelby could not speak. However, she smiled. She was so glad that her mother was with her. Ruby held her hand. It was a comforting feeling. It was the undying love between mother and child.

"We will get through it! We will get through it!"

The mother and daughter bond was renewed and was stronger than ever. Ruby knew it was going to be a hard legal battle, but she was ready to give her daughter all the moral support she would need to win.

11

Peyton dashed down the corridor to the front of the hospital. As Peyton ran, she looked only at the ground while pulling at her blonde hair.

"I am going to loose the house and the cars! I'm going to loose…"

Her sentence stopped short as she bumped into someone.

"Excuse you, holmes," a man said in a heavy Mexican accent. "God gave you a neck so you could walk with your head up, not down like a animal!"

The tone of the man's voice was familiar. When she raised her head, her heart dropped. Standing in front of her was Juan's mother and brother. Juan's mother was dressed in blue jeans and an aqua green shirt with a red scarf draped around her shoulders and Juan's brother was dressed in a black bubble coat, jeans and black boots.

"Mrs. Suarez…Rico…"

Juan's brother, Rico, voiced his anger as soon as he recognized Peyton.

"Hey, essay, it's the sneaky, sneaky little rat, holmes!"

"It's not like that…It's not like that," Peyton said.

"You shitting me, holmes! My brother gave you everything— cars, big house, and rubies! He even quit coming around us because you think we are all illegal!"

"No…No…I don't have anything against you people," Peyton

said

"What do you mean 'you people'? I ought to—"

Mrs. Suarez intervened, "Rico, watch your mouth! This is your brother's wife! Just because she has no respect doesn't mean you shouldn't."

Rico calmed down. Peyton was amazed that Mrs. Suarez took up for her.

"Mrs. Suarez, I am so sorry this has happened."

"Peyton, I am very disappointed in you, but I will not disrespect you. I've known women like you all of my life."

"Pardon me, but I don't need your criticism."

"I grew up in the slums of Mexico City where we didn't even have glass in our windows. When I met my husband, I knew that we had a chance to escape and make our lives better for our children."

"Well, you did a great job. I have to get some fresh air."

"Listen, Señora, por favor. Women like you tear men down. See, when Juan met you, he… he was so excited. He ran around the house like a kid, but, now, his heart is broken."

"Broken, holmes!" Rico added.

"Shut up, Rico before I smack you!"

Rico quieted himself as his mother finished.

"Señora, I will pray for you. I will pray that you change your ways. Now, excuse us. I have a son to tend to."

Mrs. Suarez and Rico walked past Peyton. Peyton glanced at her watch. She did not take heed of the position of its hands but of the symbolism of the device.

"I will change. It is time."

She turned back around and made her way toward the nursery. She wanted to see Itty Bitty for as long as she could.

12

In the meanwhile, Tomeka stepped outside the hospital. The day was very cold and windy. Tomeka did not hesitate. She hopped into the first available taxi.

"Timber Hill Community," Tomeka said.

The cab driver sped away as Tomeka flipped open her cell phone and called Amere Destiny. It was time to see if he had what it took to be the one.

Chapter 4
Enter The Cleanup Man

1

As he backed his black Toyota Sequoia out of Lamar's driveway, Amere called out to Lamar's father as he sat on a riding lawnmower.

"Mr. Parker, I don't know what y'all have been practicing in the backyard, but Lamar has a mean cross-over!"

"Oh yeah! We have one-on-one class every night at 7:30pm. Stop by sometime," Mr. Parker said.

"I just might. Y'all take care!"

Before he drove away, Mr. Parker and his son admired Amere's truck. His twenty-three inch chrome rims continued to spin even as he sat at a stand-still.

"Dad, I want rims like that," Lamar said.

"Son, I want your dreams to be bigger than rims. Take a good look at that man. He picks you all up, spends time with you all, and doesn't even ask for anything back."

"Yeah. He said he would order us new uniforms for a celebrity tournament in Atlanta if we show him A's and B's on our report cards."

"His dream is more than rims and playing basketball. He wants you all to be successful in life. I am thankful for him."

"Me, too. I am about to go study."

Lamar ran into his house and his dad turned the lawnmower back on. In the meanwhile, Amere's cell phone vibrated.

"I don't know that number. It could be Sherry."

Amere put the phone down at the thought. Sherry was his last girlfriend. Although she was a woman of extraordinary beauty, she was not a woman of virtue. The relationship ended when he exposed her façade of compassion. In actuality, she had diabolically sought to squander his funds in her personal real estate company. The phone vibrated a second time, but Amere did not answer it.

"Go away! I found your thongs packed between the couch cushions, a pair of pink house shoes in my walk-in closet, and a hair comb with the strands of your hair in my spare bathroom," Amere yelled at his phone.

The phone vibrated again and a simple thought occurred to him. What if it isn't Sherry? What if it is Tomeka? He picked up the phone and willed the outcome.

"No more gold diggers…No gold diggers."

Amere pulled his car onto the side of the road. He tried to practice what he preached when it came to driving while on the cell phone. He answered the phone in his soothing deep voice.

"Hello."

"Akk."

The cab driver peeped into his rearview mirror as he heard Tomeka choking. Quickly, Tomeka patted her chest and cleared her throat. She gave the cab driver an assuring thumbs-up.

"Hello?"

"Ahh. M-may I speak to Amere?"

"Who is this? I can barely hear you. Speak up."

Amere heard the caller clear her throat a second time.

"It's Tomeka from Caribbean Nights."

Amere's heart pounded in his chest. Not only was the voice as soft as rain, but it called to his lonely soul. This was the moment he had prayed for. When Amere spoke, it was hard for him to contain the cheer in his voice.

"Not the diamond princess herself? How is your day, pretty lady?"

"My day is fine."

"I asked how your day was going, not how you looked."

"Hah! You have lines."

"I have lines, quotes, and acronyms!"

Tomeka laughed. Never, throughout her two-year relationship with Antone, had she felt like she was feeling now. Amere's charm was captivating. Her cab driver pulled up at Shelby's home and opened the car door for her.

"Hold on one second, Amere. I have to pay the cabbie."

"No problem."

The cab driver got out of the car and opened the door for her.

"Thanks and keep the change," Tomeka told him as she handed her money.

Amere heard the whirring of the wind. He could hear her feet tapping the ground and a car door opening then close.

Maybe I am listening too hard...

Tomeka started her vehicle and welcomed the warm air from the heater.

"Come on, heater!"

"The hawk is out," Amere said.

"The weatherman said it would be cold and windy."

"Cold weather is only good when there is a nice fire to sit beside."

"Is that right?"

Tomeka drove her truck forward and took her time driving home. She heard a car toot its horn at Amere.

"Either you're holding up traffic or someone thinks you're cute."

"None of the above. My rims are spinning."

"They should be if you are driving."

"Well, Tomeka that's where you have me wrong."

"How do you figure?" Tomeka asked.

"I parked on the side of the road, so I could give you my undivided attention."

"That's so thoughtful of you!"

"I try."

Amere was glad. Tomeka did not even entertain the fact about his rims but focused on his considerate side. It had been a long time since she had had a conversation with a down-to-earth man. Amere felt that it was okay to proceed as planned.

"So, when are you going to come over for that steak and shrimp dinner that I offered you?"

"My signal faded in and out. Could you repeat that?" Tomeka lied.

She had never been invited to a man's house for dinner and wanted to hear the question again. Such events usually happened at her house or at a restaurant with a high health score.

"So, when are you going to come over for that steak and shrimp dinner that I offered you?" he repeated.

"Well, Chef Amere, can you have the meal ready by eight o'clock?"

"Does the sun shine on a clear day?"

"Umm, yes."

"Then, I will have the table set and the candles lit by seven-fifty! How do you like your steak and what do you want to drink?"

"I like my steak well done."

"Well done. Nothing pink."

"Unless you want me to order pizza."

"Nah. What to drink?"

"Red wine."

"Fa-sho. Fa-sho. Do you like Southwestern food?"

"Yeah, I do."

"Cool. The menu is set—Durango steak and jumbo shrimp."

"Ummm-hmm!"

"I will have the red wine on ice and the steak well done. Are you familiar with the city of Fayetteville?"

"Which end of Fayetteville? Is it the end nearest to the southern end of Clayton County around the Panhandle area or the end toward Highway 85?"

"The end near the Panhandle area. The neighborhood is Pintail Places."

"I frequently pass that neighborhood on my way to Shop-Mart. I have a friend who has family that live near there."

"I shop at Shop-Mart all the time and have never bumped into you!"

"Maybe the timing is better this time."

"Okay, Tomeka, I am going to swing by Shop-Mart and pick up some items. It is already 4:30 p.m., so can you give me a call around 6:30 p.m. to let me know if you're still coming?"

"Are you saying I am going to stand you up?"

"No, I am not speaking that into existence. I just want you to know I am flexible."

"I have had a long hectic day and a candlelit dinner would do more than turn it around. I am looking forward to our dinner date."

"Okay. Drive safely."

"You, too."

"I can't wait to see you tonight."

"I can't wait, either."

"Good-bye."

"Good-bye."

Amere clicked on his left blinker and pulled out onto the street when the coast was clear. Even though it was cold outside, Amere had the month of May. He grinned from ear to ear as he drove home. At the same time, Tomeka had high hopes for the excitement the evening would bring.

2

Fifteen minutes later, Tomeka parked her truck in her parking deck. She hurried to her elevator. When the door opened, she rushed into her home and jumped on her sofa where she laid on her back and kicked her feet in the air.

"I have a dinner date! I have a dinner date!"

She turned on the television. The commercial with Byron Smith being chased by pirates flashed on the screen. Thoughts of Byron and Peyton emerged and Tomeka wept.

"You, bastard! Why did you do this to me?"

At that moment, the cordless phone rang. Tomeka looked at the caller I.D. The area code was 504! Byron was calling her. He had no idea what she knew. Tomeka enthusiastically answered the phone as if it were a normal day.

"Hello?"

"Hey, what's up, baby girl? How's my Meka-Boo?"

"Fine."

"How is my little Janicia?"

"Looking more and more like her daddy."

"I know it's been a long time since I've seen you two, but I promise to be there during this off-season."

"I know you are busy doing everything."

Tomeka rolled her eyes.

"I know. It's crazy. Commercial here. Photo shoot there. Game time. Reporter time."

"Byron, I know it must be difficult for you."

"Yeah, well, you know the big game is tomorrow. I want you and little Janicia to fly down to check out the game from the sidelines."

Tomeka punched her pillow. It became hard to keep her composure. Peyton had not called Byron. It was an indicator for Byron to find a substitute.

"For real, Byron! You want us to come down? Are you sure?"

"Yeah, I am sure. I would love to see my two babies."

"I don't know what to say? I am so happy!"

"Maybe this will persuade you."

Byron had some romantic jazz playing in the background.

"Oh, you know my weakness."

"Come on down and I can do that thing with my mouth that you love."

"Ooooh! Don't start something you can't finish."

"I want to see your gorgeous face. The tickets will be there at the front desk."

"What hotel are you in?"

"I am in Suite 107 at The Omni Royal of New Orleans."

The last statement confirmed Juan's story. Tomeka became

silent. It was time to end this charade.

"Hello? Tomeka, are you still there?"

"Byron, it's time to end all of the smoke and mirrors."

"Huh?"

"It's over. You're busted."

"Tomeka, what are you talking about?"

"No more games, Byron. No more lies. This is your last time to come clean."

Byron became defensive.

"Clean about what? I am not taking this accusing shit off you again!"

Tomeka sat up on her couch and verbally unloaded on Byron.

"Byron, not only do I know what you did last summer, but I know who you were doing it with!"

"You're crazy. You know that?"

"Nah, I know all about you and Peyton!"

Byron winced on the other end of the phone but denied the charge.

"Peyton who? I don't know a Peyton!"

"White girl, blonde hair, tall like a model and—oh, yeah—my ex-best friend!"

"No need to get silent now! Peyton's husband found your e-mails and told me!"

"I know that you and Peyton were supposed to be together this weekend and that she was supposed to be at the game—not me, not even your own daughter!"

"Tomeka—"

"Shut up, Byron! I gave you a chance, but you tried to play stupid! What did she do to you, Byron?"

"Tomeka—"

"SHUT UP, Byron! Did she make you feel like a man? Did you think she would help your image?"

"Tomeka—"

"SHUT IT! All I ever wanted was to be a family! All I wanted was to make you feel like a father!"

"Tomeka—"

"You and I had this conversation about being a father to your child! This is very important to me. My dad passed before we could have our father-daughter dance!"

"Tomeka, please—"

"Byron, I looked at you like a father and you do this to me!"

"Peyton came on to me! It was a red-eye flight and we had just lost! What was I supposed to do?"

"Byron, you were supposed to do what was best for your daughter and me!"

"It is not that easy! If you haven't noticed, I am all over the television! I am a sex icon! People expect me to be promiscuous!"

"You're dirty, Byron! Fame has turned you into a sewer rat, a swamp fox! I am the mother of your firstborn, the beginning of your legacy!"

"It wasn't supposed to go down like this!"

"No, it wasn't, but it is what it is."

Byron swallowed. His throat was dry.

"I am sorry."

"Think about that when the first and fifteenth roll around. I better be opening an envelope with a check containing your signature."

"Baby, let's talk about this. If the paparazzi find out about you and Janicia, you won't have any privacy!"

"Byron, they are the least of your worries! Come Monday, I am going to the courthouse and put you on child support! Have a good game tomorrow!"

Tomeka hung the phone up and laid down on the couch. The conversation had drained her. She reached back and touched Janicia's teddy bear named Teddy. Actually, Teddy was the same teddy bear she used to drag around her mother's house.

"Teddy, I remember when we used to play tea."

Teddy stared back. Even over twenty years, his yarn smile had not changed.

"Teddy, maybe I should stay home and give myself some "me" time. What do you think?"

Tomeka reflected on the events and how she had met Amere. The pieces of the puzzle were on the table but she had to put them together. Staying home tonight would not create the bigger picture.

"Teddy, I think I understand what you are saying. I am going to be strong like you and go on that date tonight! Thank you, Teddy!"

She put down Teddy and walked into the bedroom. Teddy stared at her. His yarn smile did not change. It never had and it never would.

3

As Tomeka searched for the perfect outfit, Amere was stuck in the express line at the Shop-Mart on Tara Boulevard. A male customer was having problems paying with a check.

"The money isn't there, buddy," Amere said.

"I know. Well, at least we got in here when we did. The line is growing," an elderly woman said as she sat in her motor scooter in front of him. Antone glanced over his shoulder to look at the line.

"I just needed two items and this happens."

The elderly woman glanced at the six jumbo-sized chocolate dipped strawberries and two scented candles.

"Either you have a sweet tooth or you have a date."

"I have a date."

"She must be special."

"We just met, but I hope we can get to know how special we both are."

"Find out about her mother and dad. If they good, she good."

"The apple doesn't fall too far from the tree, huh?"

"No sir. I tell my grandson that it is okay to go out to eat 'cause you got to eat but don't be paying those women's bills and you go lacking!'

Amere laughed aloud. The man finally paid for his items. The line moved forward.

"Your grandson is two steps ahead."

"These no good girls are smart! They have a baby with a good man and that's a paycheck!"

"The guy feels trapped because if he don't pay, he goes to jail!"

"Yes, sir! Then, they live on the fat of the land! These days, folks don't have children to survive. They have children for fun!"

"You're right, but men are just as bad."

"They are, but you ain't interested in men, are you?"

Amere quickly shook his head.

"No! I love women!"

"Okay, then listen! A good woman is good all the way through. She will have some scars and dents—she ain't perfect! Do you understand?"

"Yes ma'am."

"She ain't perfect but she good because she has been through the bad to appreciate something that's good!

"Preach!"

"Now, if this young lady you just met ain't been through the bad—bad over, bad behind, what you gone do?"

"I am going to be patient."

"Hell, nawh! You leave her ass alone! It's too many fish in the sea! Now, if you don't mind, help me put my groceries up."

"I'll do more than that, I will pay for them," Amere said.

"Baby, you good. I hope she good!"

Amere hugged the elderly lady and assisted her with her groceries. Four people behind him stood his ex-girlfriend, Sherry Ashburn. She was dressed in a gray two-piece suit with a white camisole beneath the jacket. A skinny white guy was moved by Amere's actions.

"That's a nice guy. He is paying for that old lady's food. Can I buy your bottle of ketchup for you?"

"Do I look like I need charity?"

Once a week, Sherry drove one hour from Lawrenceville to Jonesboro in hopes of following Amere back to his home. Each time she visited Shop-Mart at Tara Boulevard, she purchased one item. After the break-up and the financial ruin of her real-estate company, Sherry forgot how to get to Amere's house. Today was the day of reckoning she had been waiting for.

4

Sherry watched as Amere helped the elderly lady load her groceries onto the counter. After they were wrung up, he paid for them. Anger boiled within her.

"He helps old ladies with their groceries but won't help finance my company..." Sherry contemplated.

Sherry watched Amere put his items on the counter. There were two scented candles and a six-pack of chocolate dipped strawberries.

"Someone is having a romantic dinner tonight. There will be love making by the fireplace…"

She watched as Amere pushed the elderly lady's groceries out the store. Sherry waited and then dropped the bottle of ketchup in the guy's basket behind to her.

"Hey! You said you didn't want charity!"

"One dollar and nineteen cents plus tax. I buy a bottle every week."

Sherry stormed out the door and put on a pair of black shades. She searched around and whispered to herself, "Where are you, Amere?"

Suddenly, she saw Amere trotting from the elderly woman's car back to his black truck. Sherry dashed to her teal green Kompressor that was parked in handicapped parking. As Amere cruised past, Sherry followed behind him.

"This is your last sunset, Amere. Enjoy it."

Sherry followed Amere. She planned to shoot him down as soon as he stepped out of his car in his front yard.

5

While he waited to make a left turn onto Tara Road, Amere flipped through his CD booklet in search of something to listen to. He browsed and came across the Master P classic "TRU Disc One". He put the disc in and skipped to track listing number two as he made his turn. Moby D soulfully sang:

"I always feel like somebody's watching me…"

Amere bounced his head to Master P's rowdy lyrics as he rapped about being chased through his neighborhood. The driver in front of Amere flipped on his left blinker and prepared to turn into a subdivision as soon as oncoming traffic passed. Amere slowed down and glanced in his left side mirror.

"It can't be! It can't be!"

One car behind him, he saw a green Kompressor. Even more frightening was seeing the light-skinned woman behind the steering wheel.

"I always feel like someone's watching me..."

"Maybe she didn't see me."

Amere turned his steering wheel to the left. Sherry saw the front wheel turn. She extended her middle finger and then whisked it beneath her chin.

"Go ahead and make my day!"

"Damn! She saw me!"

Amere swerved his vehicle around the driver in front of him and accelerated down the byway. Suddenly, there was the sound of tires screaming and horns blaring.

"SSKRRR!"

Amere looked in his mirror and saw Sherry swerve into oncoming traffic. Horns blared.

"Watch out! Are you crazy?!"

Within a couple of seconds, Sherry was behind him flashing her lights off and on.

"I'll loose her in this neighborhood!"

Amere swerved right and entered the large subdivision known as BONANZA. Behind him, Sherry locked on her brakes as she made the tight turn.

"You should have given me that loan, Amere! I only needed one-hundred thousand dollars!"

Sherry reached into her glove compartment and pulled out her loaded automatic pistol. She leaned out the side of her window and took aim. Amere made another sharp right hand turn.

BLAM!

Amere ducked in the driver's seat!

"What was that?"

He looked behind him! Shattered glass was all over his back seat!

"She shot my back window out!"

Amere mashed the gas. A blind man could shoot his large vehicle. Thoughts raced through his mind. If Sherry had the nerve to blast out his car window, she would kill him.

"I have one chance! I can't outrun a V-12, but I can make her miss!"

Amere jerked his steering wheel from left to right. Sherry fired again!

BLAM! BLAM!

The gunshots missed, but Amere continued to drive half-ducking down. Deftly, Amere pulled out his cell phone and called 911. The phone rang once and the operator quickly picked up the phone.

"Clayton County 911. I am Operator 35. How may I assist you?"

"My name is Amere Destiny! I am on my way to the police precinct on the edge of BONANZA! There is a crazy lady shooting at me in a Kompressor! Call for back up!"

"Sir, calm down."

BLAM!

Another bullet shattered Amere's side mirror as he veered right.

"Did you hear that? I can't be calm when someone is shooting at me!"

"What type of vehicle are you in?

"I am in a black Toyota Sequoia! Have the police at the precinct to meet me!"

Amere pressed the gas as he made a sharp left and sped toward the South Clayton Precinct. Suddenly, a round gunfire of exploded!

BLAM! BLAM! BLAM! BLAM!

"Damn! She got my tires! She got my tires!"

Amere's vehicle swerved out of control as his rims ground against the asphalt. The acrid smoke from his wheel's stung his eyes as he swerved his vehicle into the shopping center where the police station was located.

"Where are the police? Where are they?"

The sun shot its last rays of sunlight over the land as his truck came to a halt. Amere stared into his rearview mirror. Sherry's car slowly rolled through the smoke. Immediately, Amere slid into the passenger seat and contemplated.

When she pulls up, I will jump out of the opposite side and run as fast as I can... Lord, be with me!!!

Sherry smiled as she studied her handy work. The SUV was slumped to the side and riddled with bullet holes. Now, she put her car in park. It was time to finish what was started. She put on her black shades and stepped outside her vehicle.

"It's a good day to shoot someone you used to love."

Sherry rubbed the barrel of her pistol and noticed a red dot on her hand.

"What in the—"

"Freeze! Don't move! Put your weapon down!"

The captain of the SWAT team popped out of an adjacent wooded area with his pistol extended.

SKKRR!

Sherry wheeled around at the sound of skidding tires.

"What! How?"

Two black SWAT team cars quickly blocked off the street. The officers leapt out with their pistols drawn. More SWAT team members rushed from around the corner of a nearby building. The area was secured and Sherry was out smarted.

"It's over! Put your weapon down! You are completely surrounded by land and air!"

The sound of a black helicopter was heard approaching.

"It's never over!" Sherry shouted.

She pointed the pistol to her head.

"I'll do it! I'll do it!'

The SWAT members stood their ground. A gusty breeze blew and streamed through her jet-black hair. For a moment, the scene could have been mistaken for a neo shampoo commercial.

"Get back! I am not going to jail to be some hairy woman's sex slave!"

"Lady, put your gun down! It is over! It is over!"

"No! No! Burn, Amere!" Sherry screamed.

She wheeled and fired toward Amere's gas tank.

BLAM! BLAM!

Amere leapt out of the truck, grabbed his grocery bag, and ran for his life.

BOOM!

Amere was hurled to the ground by the force of the explosion. Sherry trotted toward Amere with her pistol extended. Amere begged for his life.

"It's not worth it, Sherry."

"What I am going to do is worth it! All you had to do was give me the one hundred thousand!"

"Think about what you are doing."

Sherry stood over Amere. A tear trickled from Amere's left eye.

"I already did. Good bye!"

CLICK! CLICK!

The SWAT team members did not hesitate. He knelt and yelled.

"Take her down!"

BLAM! BLAM!

Amere watched as Sherry fell to the ground.

"EMS, send an ambulance and a fire engine to the southern entrance of the South Clayton Police Precinct along with a flat bed truck. Signal five," the captain of the SWAT team reported.

"We copy, Ground Hog. FireFly and Ladybug are en route. Signal five," the EMS operator replied.

The captain of the SWAT team assisted Amere to his feet. Amere could hear the blaring sirens of the approaching ambulance. Amere read the nametag on the captain's vest.

"Thanks, Captain Flates."

"It's a miracle you are alive, son."

"I thought she was going to shoot me dead."

Captain Flates stooped down and picked up Sherry's pistol. He cocked the pistol and popped a bullet out of the chamber.

"You should be dead. She squeezed the trigger twice. God was with you!"

"Thank you, God!"

Another SWAT member walked up to Amere.

"Are you injured?"

"Um, no, I am fine. Just a little shaken."

"Check him. He is pumping adrenaline," Captain Flates ordered.

After a moment, Amere was cleared. He had no injuries.

"Captain Flates, what do I need to fill out? I am supposed to have dinner ready by eight o'clock."

"You can still make the appointment, little Emeril. The fire department is going to clean this mess up," Captain Flates said.

"Okay, can I get a ride to my house? I stay down the street in the lakeside community of 10712 Pintail Places."

"Affirmative. That is a very nice neighborhood. I want to move there when I retire."

Captain Flates yelled over the noise.

"C, Twelve, Francois, and, Trav, keep those people back!"

Immediately, the SWAT members secured the area from the curious pedestrians. Captain Flates studied Amere. He was clean-cut, healthy-looking, and well-rounded.

"You seem like a nice guy. How did you get caught up in this?"

"Sherry used to be my girlfriend until I found out that she was scheming to use my money to save her realty company."

"How long did you date?"

"One month!"

"What a nut case! I have been dating my ole lady for ten years and we haven't had any problems!"

"Yeah, what a nut case."

Amere didn't know who was more of a nut case, Sherry or Captain Flates live-in wife. Captain Flates grabbed Amere by the arm and led him to one of the waiting cars. They sped off. The dinner was still on!

6

Tomeka gazed at herself in her full-length mirror. She was

dressed in a beaded wine-colored silk cocktail dress with spaghetti straps. The dress accented her collarbone and cleavage.

"Amere, you are not going have a chance to say any form of the word "no" when you see me," Tomeka said.

She put her diamond studs in her ears and a platinum bracelet on her wrist. Tomeka slid on a pair of Italian black leather slides with a 2 ¼" heel. Tomeka quickly transferred her driver's license to a purse with two large gold ring handles. She glanced at the digital clock. It was time to make her phone call.

"Hello?"

"Hey, Amere. It's Tomeka. Um, what's that noise?"

"Oh. I'm just stepping out the shower."

"You're naked!"

"Um, not anymore. I am drying off."

"I can't be having these thoughts."

"Yes, you can. Martin made this a free country."

"Whew! Cold water! Cold water!"

Tomeka fanned herself. All of sudden, it had become hot in her condo.

"If this makes you feel any better, I have boxers on now."

"Let's change the subject. How was your day?"

"Well, it was a day like no other. It is one of those things that I have to tell you about in person. Do you still remember how to get here?"

"Yeah, Mr. Destiny. You wouldn't believe my day either. We can definitely talk about this in person."

"That's what up. Remember to take Tara Boulevard to Tara Road to McDonough Road."

"Got it. What do I do when I enter the neighborhood?"

"When you get to the front gate, enter the code 725 to open it. Take the main road until it becomes a bridge over the lake. After you cross over the lake, you will pass the clubhouse and my house will be the first brick house on the right. The name of that street is Woodcock Manor."

"Gotcha. I will be there in about half an hour or so."

"Okay. I am going to make sure the food is ready. Drive safe."

"I will. Good-bye."

"Good-bye.

The call ended and Tomeka walked to her closet and chose a smoke gray chinchilla jacket. She reflected on where she had come in the last two days. She had gone from deeply depressed to greatly impressed! It was funny how quickly tables turned. Hopefully, her table had turned from the back row to the front seat on the center stage.

7

Amere brushed his teeth and rinsed with a capful of mouthwash. He put lotion on his muscular arms and hands as well. He did not want to shake Tomeka's hand and have her see him ashy. Next, he slipped on a pair of black designer jeans, a baby blue French collar shirt, and a black blazer with a suede collar. Amere looked in the mirror.

"This is why I'm hot! This is why I'm hot! Now, it's time for the anointing," Amere chanted.

Amere sprayed his neck, arms, and pants with his cologne. Amere rushed down his winding stairs. Quickly, he decorated his dining room table. The table sat on a three-foot tall marble dais. Beside the table was a bay window that overlooked the lake. There was a wine colored tablecloth, two twelve-inch dinner candles, two plates, utensils that were wrapped in napkins, and two saucers.

"Now, that's how you set a table! Now, where are the champagne glasses?"

Amere grabbed a bottle of red wine and placed it in the thick glass bucket. He surrounded the bottle of wine with ice and set the bucket of ice near the table. Amere leaned on the table and beseeched the one who made all things possible.

"Lord, I am thankful to you for bringing this young lady into my life. You have guided me and protected me. I pray that you bless this dinner as a new beginning. Amen. Amen. Amen."

The prayer rejuvenated him. Tonight would be the beginning of something special.

8

There was little or no traffic as Tomeka cruised south on Interstate-75 toward Tara Boulevard. She was hungry and prepared to call for carryout pizza if Amere's steak was burnt. She exited onto Tara Boulevard, a street notorious for cops swooping down out of nowhere and giving you a ticket.

"The trusty radar detector has not detected any po pos,' Tomeka said.

After a while, Tomeka turned right onto Tara Rd. Suddenly, her phone rang. She answered it.

"Hello."

"Tomeka, I am so sorry."

Tomeka frowned when she realized that it was Byron calling her.

"Byron, have you been crying?"

"Yes. My eyes are swelling."

"Good. Go take some Benedryl and some Visine. I have to go!"

"Baby, I know you are mad. I messed up. I lov—"

Tomeka interrupted Byron.

"That's where you messed up when you thought you loved me!"

"Tomeka—"

"Do we have anything to discuss about Janicia?"

"Tomeka—"

"I thought so."

Tomeka ended the phone call and tossed her phone into to the armrest compartment as she turned onto McDonough Road. Tomeka rounded the corner and entered the gated community of 10712 Pintail Places.

"Those are some beautiful trees!"

Tomeka marveled at the towering pines, the lush cedars, and Colorado spruces that bordered the road.   She pulled up to a large gate and entered the code that Amere had given her. The iron-gate opened and she drove into the community. She crossed a bridge that stretched across an enormous lake.

"Wow. The lake looks like a sea?"

Tomeka could see lights twinkling in the distance. The view was breathtaking. Tomeka passed the clubhouse and turned onto Woodcock Manor.

"Now, where is the h…"

Tomeka cut her sentence short as Amere's house came into view on a hilltop. It was a miniature Victorian-style home with a three-car garage.

"That's not a house. That is a palace!"

Tomeka drove up the winding driveway. Just then, the middle door of the triple-door garage opened up for her to enter. Amere was standing in the gap.

9

Amere watched Tomeka step out of her vehicle. She was dressed to kill. Tomeka looked around the garage. There was a black Humvee with yellow accents and a midnight black ninja motorcycle. Amere pressed a button to close the garage.

"What's that look for?" Tomeka asked.

"I need to pinch myself."

"Why do you need to do that, Amere?"

"Because I must be dreaming."

"And what if you are?"

"If I am, then I hope that no one wakes me!"

Amere hugged Tomeka. Tomeka's toes curled as she rubbed her hands across Amere's broad shoulders.

"You look very nice," Tomeka said.

"Thank you. You are as gorgeous as ever."

"You smell good, too."

"Come on. Let's go inside. I have something that smells better."

Amere took her hand and entered the home.

"Welcome to Casa de Destiny," Amere said.

"Wow! It is amazing!"

"Thanks. This is the middle level. Below, is a bar, game room, and theater."

"Amere, I love your winding stairs. It's like something out of a movie."

Amere led Tomeka into an adjacent room.

"This is the library. Over there, where you see the blue and orange couches, is my showcase room where I keep my trophies."

"A trophy case? Did you play football?"

"No, but I am a beast at foosball. I was a basketball kid. I played for the Atlanta Fire Cats until my accident."

"I remember you! I heard one of my friends talking about that! I am glad to see you recovered!"

"Thanks. It was hard, but I did it. Now, let's go to the dining room. I'm starved!"

After a few twists and turns, they entered the dining room.

"Your jacket, my lady?"

"Of course."

Amere took Tomeka's jacket and purse and hung them up in a nearby closet. Amere was such a gentleman.

"Could I use your restroom so I can wash my hands?" Tomeka asked.

"Yeah. Go straight down the hall. There is one on the right."

Amere watched and admired Tomeka's runway walk.

"Lord, you knew what you were doing when you put grace in a woman's walk," Amere whispered.

Amere lit the fireplace and dimmed the lights. He lit the dinner and scented candles and began to set the table. Then, Amere turned on some light jazz. The climate was set for romance to blossom. Tomeka returned from the bathroom and was impressed. Amere helped Tomeka up the small steps of the dais and into her seat.

"So, is this how you treat every woman you meet at your club?" Tomeka asked.

"Oh, no! Some people never make it to the front gate! At the first site of any drama, Amere does a magic trick...poof, he's gone!"

"That is the least of your worries. My drama is gone," Tomeka said.

"That guy at the club...I believe you said his name was Antone."

"Yeah, what about him?"

"Is he…"

Tomeka softly touched Amere's hand.

"Amere, I wouldn't be here if Antone was still in the picture. It's just us three."

Amere looked left and right.

"Who…Who's the third person?"

Tomeka smiled. Amere thought that her smile was so pretty.

"Me, you, and good ole opportunity!"

Amere laughed as he took the plates and walked away.

"You got me! You got me!"

Amere returned with a tray of steaming food. Tomeka trashed the contingency plan of ordering pizza. The food smelled so good that it had to be good!

"Oh! I can't wait to eat! How did you do this? I have never had yellow Mexican rice!"

"I sautéed these jumbo shrimp with the vegetables and grilled our steak with pepper sauce. Also, I put a light mix of melted cheese, cilantro, and rajas over the steak. I hope you like it."

Amere set the food down and popped the cork of the chilled red wine.

POP!

Amere poured the red wine into the two fluted glasses. Then, Amere sat down and reached across the table. Tomeka placed her hands in his. She knew what he was about to do. It was something she had always wanted to do with the man in her life.

"Let us bow our heads and give thanks for this meal."

She bowed her head and concentrated as Amere prayed over the food in his deep voice.

"Father God, who are in heaven, thank you for this meal that has been prepared for us today. Thank you for bringing Tomeka and me together for this dinner. She told me that today was a bad day and I, too, had a bad day, but we can't count any day as a bad day until all our days have been called in! Jesus, we would like to thank you for being with us through these troubling times, giving us strength, and carrying us when we could not stand on our own. Please, bless this food and thank you again for this meal. Amen. Amen. Amen."

Tomeka released Amere's hands and unfolded her napkin. She placed her silverware on the table and the napkin in her lap. As she spoke, her voice was slow but amazed, "I have never had a man to pray over my food."

"I hope that I didn't offend you. I didn't even ask your religion."

"No, I was not offended! I love the Lord, I love Jehovah, I love Jesus, and I love everything in the Bible!"

"Whew! That is one thing that can split two people apart. The other thing is politics!"

"True. One thing I have learned in life is that prayer is good!"

"What church do you attend?"

"I attend Philadelphia Baptist Church in Hampton, Georgia."

"I know exactly where your church is."

"Yeah, it is just your average small church. The preacher knows everyone in his congregation."

"I've visited there once or twice and each time the message was good. The praying made me want to pray all the time!"

"It's hard to find a man who prays."

"Tomeka, I am not going to pretend I am perfect. I have my flaws like any other Joe, but I try my best to live by the golden rule."

"Do unto others as you would have them do unto you."

"Yep, but it's a struggle when people treat you bad."

Tomeka started to cut her steak into small cubes.

"I feel ya. It seems like my entire life is a struggle and I am tired of struggling with people trying to walk over me."

"Struggling is only temporary. Your time is coming."

Tomeka nodded her head. They started dining on the meal. It wasn't long before Tomeka complimented his cooking.

"This…is better than good! How did you learn to cook like this?!"

Amere sipped his wine before answering.

"Being by yourself teaches you plenty. At one point in my life, I was eating out everyday."

"That's unhealthy, Amere."

"Same thing my doctor said. So I learned how to cook home-cooked meals with all the trimmings."

"You must get lonely staying here by yourself."

"I do. The saying is true, 'The most important things in a house are the people'."

Tomeka squinted at Amere.

"Are you trying to imply something?"

Amere laughed aloud.

"It the shoes fits, walk a thousand miles in them!"

Tomeka smiled as she shook her head. Amere watched as she speared the cube of meat then guided it to her mouth. He knew that she could be the one. She could be the one who steals my heart.

"Amere, you are spoiling me."

"What makes you say that?"

"Don't you know what happens when demand passes supply in economic terms?"

"Are you implying I am going to have to cook more for you?"

"Exactly!"

"Let's finish eating before we talk big business."

Amere and Tomeka continued to eat. Every once in a while, Tomeka would glance upward at Amere and smile.

10

Tomeka finished her meal and pushed her plate to the side. She was stuffed but still curious. She wanted to know more about Amere Destiny. Why would someone of his caliber have a bad day?

"So, tell me why your day was so bad?"

"Let me see. My car was shot up until it exploded and a girl I used to date was killed today."

"What?"

"Yeah, we had dated for a month. I found out she was trying to take money from me to fund her business that was folding, so I broke it off."

"Wow."

"Yeah, so she finally tracked me down and shot up my truck! In the end, the SWAT team had to take her down."

"Unbelievable!"

"You're telling me! It all went down after I came out of Shop-Mart after talking to you."

Tomeka leaned back in her chair and crossed her arms.

"And you still made dinner for me, after all of this happened?"

"I was made for this."

Tomeka blushed as Amere cleared the dinner table.

"Thank you for the food. It was very delicious."

"You're welcome and thank you for coming. I hope you have room for dessert."

Amere disappeared and returned with a saucer of chocolate

dipped strawberries. Tomeka took a bite of the delicacy. It almost felt like heaven.

"This is so good, Amere."

"So, what made your day so bad?"

"Today I discovered that one of my best friends had overdosed after finding out her husband had gotten another lady pregnant."

"What! Is she okay?"

"Yeah, I found her just in time. Oh, it gets better."

"There is more?"

"I discovered my other best friend has been sleeping with my baby's father!"

"Are you okay?"

"Yeah, my baby's father is Byron Smith."

"Byron Smith, as in the Touchdown King!"

"Well, I know him as "Mr. Asshole". We have a four-year-old daughter, named Janicia, who he never wants to be around, even in his off-season."

"That is bad. If I am rewarded with the chance to meet your daughter, I promise to make the best of the experience."

"First, you have to earn my trust."

"Then, I will start tonight."

Amere picked up a chocolate-covered strawberry, knelt before Tomeka, and fed it to her. He watched as her teeth penetrated the chocolate coating and her lips enveloped the fruit. Not a drop of juice escaped those lips.

"Tomeka, your lips look so soft."

"Why should they look soft? Why don't you tell me how soft they are?"

Tomeka leaned forward and kissed Amere. They felt each other's tongues and tasted each other's beings. Amere's hands moved along Tomeka's body from hips to breasts. She didn't just like it; she loved it!

"Amere...Amere, do you promise..."

"I promise never to betray you."

Amere scooped Tomeka from her seat in his massive arms without breaking their passionate connection. He carried Tomeka up the stairs to his master bedroom and gently laid Tomeka on his bed. As they rolled from side to side, clothing disappeared.

"Tomeka...Tomeka, are you ready for this?"

"Amere...I was made for this!"

Tomeka unbuttoned his shirt and kissed along the lines of his hard chest.

"Oh! Your chest is so hard! Thank God you work-out!"

"Tonight, you are going to work-out with me," Amere replied.

Amere unzipped Tomeka's dress and slowly undressed her down to her black thong. Amere turned Tomeka onto her back.

"Amere, what...what are you doing?" she moaned.

"I am taking a trip downtown."

He kissed her around her navel and inner hips. Tomeka's toes curled as she felt Amere's soft lips press against her inner thigh.

Amere gave her the best mouth and lip service she had ever received.

"Ohhh... Ohhh... Mmm...Ahh... Ahh...Uhhh...Amere... Ohhh..."

Tomeka clutched the back of Amere's wavy head as she felt his warm tongue.

"Amere...Amere...I want you."

"Tomeka...I am yours!"

Amere slipped off his shirt and jeans. He pressed play on his remote control that operated his stereo. The sounds of Avant's "Don't Say No, Just Say Yes" resonated throughout the room.

"One second, Tomeka."

"What are you doing?"

Then, Amere opened the top drawer of his nightstand and took out a condom in a gold wrapper.

"No love without the glove," Amere said.

"Come and give it to me, big daddy. This is all yours."

"Don't say...No...(Just Say)...Yes...Oh way...your body's what I need," Avant sang.

Amere slid between Tomeka's thighs. They made the best love that two could have ever made.

11

Tomeka awoke from a deep sleep at 6:45 on Sunday morning. She was very thirsty.

How many orgasms did I have? I've never been thirsty after sex before, Tomeka wondered.

She pulled her wild hair back. Next to her, Amere slept on his side. On his right shoulder was a tattoo of the state of Georgia and the words 'Georgia Boy'.

Every Georgia Boy needs a Georgia Girl!

Tomeka turned. Then, she turned back around. After a performance like last night, it was hard for her to take her eyes off of Amere, be away from him, or lose him to anyone else. However, she had to go to church. Her child was expecting her.

I'm coming Janicia.

Tomeka slid out of the bed and got dressed. By the time she was fully dressed it was 7:15. She found a notebook, pulled out a blank sheet of paper, and wrote Amere a message:

Dear Amere,

Thank you for the great time last night. Thank you for the food and thank you for being you. I am glad we met. I have to go to my home church in Hampton and pick up my daughter, Janicia. I will be looking forward to hearing from you. Maybe we can hook up later on today.

Until then,

Tomeka

Tomeka put on some red lipstick and kissed the paper. She placed the message on the pillow where she had slept, tiptoed down the steps, and entered the garage. She pressed the button to open the garage and backed her car out the driveway. Then, she pressed the button to close the garage. Tomeka scuttled under the closing garage.

"Good bye, Amere."

Tomeka blew Amere a kiss as she drove away. She picked up her cell phone and checked her messages.

"Greetings, Tomeka! You have one urgent message received at 1:00 a.m. Press one to hear the current message...two..."

Pressing the appropriate number on the keypad, she listened attentively.

"Tomeka...I feel like shit...I mean...I wish I could be the man I should be and not this scum...I don't know if I am going to play in the game on Sunday...my head is so messed up...I want to see you and little J…when you get this message please call me…okay talk to you later."

Tomeka deleted the message. She hated that it had to come to this for Byron to humble himself. However, if Byron had changed his ways earlier, this would be the perfect chance for her to be a family but that would mean Amere would be tossed out the picture.

"Man, I am so confused! Lord, help me! Don't let me mess up!"

Tomeka had a decision to make. Hopefully, she would not make the wrong one.

12

At 9:15 a.m., Amere rolled over on his back and his right hand touched thin air.

"What in the…Tomeka?"

She was gone. The intense love-making had put him in a deep sleep. Now, Amere looked around. On the pillow next to him, he found a handwritten message.

"She signed the message with her lip print," Amere observed.

As he read each word, he could distinctly hear Tomeka's voice dictating along.

'I can hear her voice in my head! I am whupped!"

Amere read the short message twice and became inspired to do something spontaneous for Tomeka.

"What can I do to make her have a good day? She has such a good heart."

Moments passed. Then, it dawned on him what he could do. He rushed to his walk-in closet and picked out a black Italian suit and square-toe shoes.

"Today, I am going to church, but first…"

Amere hopped in the shower. Before he made it to church, he would have to make a stop.

13

After she finished cleaning up her abode so that her daughter could return to a nice clean home, Tomeka took a long, steamy, relaxing shower and wrangled in the hair that Amere had lovingly messed up.

"Dang, Amere! You almost made me sweat my perm out!"

Tomeka brushed her teeth and slipped on a black conservative pinstriped jacket with a pair of calfskin pumps.

"Pearls for the girls," Tomeka said as she snapped on a pearl necklace and pearl bracelet watch. She slipped on her long black coat and picked up her purse. As she drove south on Interstate-75, she reflected on Byron's message.

"Am I blowing my chance to have a family, my chance of finally being happy?" Tomeka asked as she passed an eighteen-wheeler.

"Janicia barely even knows Byron."

Tomeka passed a mini-van.

"What if he comes in our lives and leave again?"

Byron's record spoke for itself. He had always put her and Janicia second, third, or fourth on his things to do list.

"What if Amere doesn't want what I want? What if he wakes up one day and doesn't want to be a father."

Tomeka exited the interstate and drove for about ten minutes. She pulled into the church driveway and passed the sign that read "Philadelphia Baptist Church welcomes all visitors". Tomeka parked in the third row of the parking lot. She stepped out her truck and stared at the L-shaped building that was her spiritual home. The mass choir was singing so loud that Tomeka could hear them in the parking lot.

"Mrs. Frances knows how to whip a choir into shape."

Tomeka walked up the steps and entered the church. She stood in the foyer of the church and listened to the melodic sounds of Philadelphia's mass choir.

Jesus is a rock...In a weary land...
In a weary land...In a weary land
Jesus is a rock...In a weary land...
And a shelter in the time of a storm...
Tomeka Washington had returned to the House of the Lord.

14

As Tomeka entered her church, Amere trotted out of Southlake Mall with two small bags in his hand—one from Friedman's Jewelers and the other from Hallmark. Pushing a loaded cart beside him was a worker from the toy department store.

"Can you take it out of the box and just place it in the back of my truck?" Amere asked.

The wind blasted against them!

"Yes, that will be no problem! Man, I need a hat!"

Puffs of white air issued from the worker's moutth. Amere pressed the remote on his key chain.

The motorized trunk of his Humvee opened and the engine started.

"That is hot! A motorized trunk," the worker yelled over the car's engine.

"I appreciate that. I got the idea from a car show last year."

"The one at the motor speedway?"

"Yeah.

"I am going this year."

The cold wind blasted them again. Amere checked his watch.
He was running late.

"I've got to go. Take these twenty dollars and get you a tam."

Amere hopped into the Humvee and turned the heater on. Behind
him, the worker loaded the item in the trunk. He rushed to the door
and handed Amere a pair of pink keys.

"Your k-keys, sir. I-I will get me a hat. I hope your little girl
enjoys. Thanks."

"Thanks. Me, too."

Amere rolled up his window and left the parking lot. Hopefully,
this gift would help bridge them together. In minutes, he was on the
expressway headed south.

"I am coming, Tomeka. I am coming."

If things went as planned, his days of loneliness would soon be
a thing of the past.

15

Tomeka entered the crowded church and walked down the red-
carpeted aisle to the second row of burgundy plush pews where her
mother sat. She saw her mother sitting beside Mrs. Ellen. The two
large speakers positioned in the middle of the thirty-foot vaulted
ceiling provided wonderful acoustics, giving Mrs. Frances and the
mass choir a high quality sound.

Jesus is a rock...In a weary land...

In a weary land...In a weary land

Jesus is a rock...In a weary land...

And a shelter in the time of a storm...

When Tomeka reached the end of the second row, Mrs. Ellen hugged her. Mrs. Ellen was dressed in a creamy white dress with a black studded creamy white hat. It was the same Mrs. Ellen who was friends with Shelby's family.

"Hey, Mrs. Ellen," Tomeka whispered.

"Hey, baby. I want you to stay strong now. Things are already better than you know."

"Yes, ma'am."

Tomeka slid past Mrs. Ellen and sat between her daughter and her mother. Janicia was dressed in a white dress with pink ribbons and her mother was dressed in a gray suit. The choir lowered their song to a soul-soothing hum as the ushers came to take up a benevolent offering.

"Momma, you were almost late," Janicia whispered in her tiny voice.

"I know. Give Mommy a kiss."

Tomeka leaned over and Janicia kissed her on the cheek. Tomeka then smiled at her mom.

"Hey, mom."

"Hey, baby. Pay me back later," Natalie said as she dropped ten dollars into the money tray as it passed her way.

The choir continued to hum. A baldheaded man stood up from his seat on the first row of the deacon board. He was dressed in a navy blue suit and slightly bent from age.

"Mom, is Deacon Scott still praying?" Tomeka asked.

"Yes, he hasn't missed a beat! Reverend Life still takes him to different churches to help set the mood."

"Isn't he about seventy-five? "

"But still moving like he's twenty-five!"

They watched as he stood before the table where the tithes and offerings were to be placed so that they could be prayed over. In a matter of minutes, the ushers placed the stuffed money trays on the table and returned to their positions along the walls. Everyone in the congregation bowed their heads as Deacon Scott cleared his throat and spoke in a powerful voice.

"Father God of Abraham, Isaac, and Jacob, thank you for waking us up in our right minds this morning," Deacon Scott prayed.

"Yes, Lord," the congregation responded.

"Thank you for giving us the strength to make it to your house this morning, Precious Lawd! Please bless those who contributed as well as those who had a mind to give but could not."

The choir continued to hum.

"Thank you for guiding us over, thy Great Jehovah, this river of Jordan! Halle-Halleee-Hallejuah!"

"Yes, Lord!" Someone shouted out from the mother board.

"Thank you, Jesus!"

Tomeka recognized the voice. It belonged to a lady named Ms. Patsy. If tradition held, she would shout today.

"Philadelphia, the storm is passing over!"

"It's almost over," Ms. Patsy shouted.

"Bless those, God of David, who have no food in their cupboard and water barely dripping from their sinks! Let them know that you are a provider whose supply never gets used up! Howdy, Howdy and Never Goodbye!"

"Thank you, Jesus! Thank you, Jesus!" Ms. Patsy exclaimed.

"Let them know that you are a doctor and a counselor! Bless this contribution to be used for those who have lost their jobs and are struggling to keep the lights on! Let them know you are the light!"

Ms. Patsy began to shout as she caught the spirit. She danced around as she shouted. The ushers rushed over to keep her from causing any injury to herself or others.

"He did it! God helped me! He heard me!"

"Bless this contribution to be used for those who need help! Bless those who have been used and abused! Free those who are confused! Howdy, Howdy and Never Goodbye! Amen! Amen! Amen!"

Deacon Scott's words beat down on Tomeka. Shouts of praises came from every corner of the building.

"Thank you, Jesus!"

"Yes, Lord!"

"Praise your name!"

"Hallelujah!"

Tomeka opened her eyes. The ushers were rushing to assist with the people who were shouting with joy. Ms. Patsy's sister, Ruth, was trying to hold her waving hands. Once the ushers had regained control of the situation, Ms. Frances stood and led the mass choir with the selection, "Oh, Happy Day".

Oh, happy day...oh, happy day...

Oh, happy day...oh, happy day

When Jesus washed...oh when he washed...

He washed my sins away...oh, happy day...

Tomeka swayed from right to left in her seat as she clapped her hands to the uplifting music of the mass choir. She felt refreshed and was glad that she had come to church.

16

Amere leapt up the stairs of the church. As he entered the foyer of the church, Amere could hear Deacon Scott's prayer. He sat in a nearby chair and waited until the prayer was over to enter the church.

"Yes, Lord," Amere said.

Deacon Scott's words were powerful and seemed to complete him. Amere glanced at a nearby bulletin board with pictures of family members. The feeling for him to belong to a family was stronger than ever.

"Lord, your ways are perfect. I know that I met this young lady for a reason. I trust your will. Let it be done," Amere said.

When the prayer was over, he stood and entered the sanctuary. As Amere took a seat in the back row, he caught a glimpse of Tomeka sitting on the second pew.

"Is that...yeah, that's Tomeka!"

The choir finished their song and the man of God rose from his seat. He was dressed in a black two-piece suit and had a neatly styled afro. Amere looked on the program for the preacher's name. It was Reverend E. Life. He stepped to the podium and addressed the church in his deep, soul-moving voice.

"Good morning, church."

"Good morning," the congregation replied.

"Thank you, Deacon Scott, for the powerful prayer that you just administered. Man should always pray, the Bible says. I always say if you worry, you didn't pray; if you pray, you don't worry."

"That's what my mom always said," Amere whispered.

"Thank you, mass choir, for the selections. To the first lady, Sister Life; my fellow brothers in the ministry, Reverend Crews and Reverend Gaston; and the unified congregation of Philadelphia Baptist Church."

Amere sat on the edge of his seat. Something called out to him.

"Friends in Christ, last night I had a sermon well-prepared and filled with scriptures but on my way here today, I decided to preach that another day."

Reverend E. Life closed his Holy Bible and adjusted his silver rimmed glasses. He leaned on the podium and peered out into the crowd. A hush fell on the people as they waited for the message.

"As I rode from Atlanta down to Philadelphia Baptist, I thought about all of the mess on television, on the radio, and how it manifests in people's lives today as adversity. Philadelphia, this world is full of illusions, confusions, and mirages that lead nowhere."

"Tell it! Tell it!" Deacon Scott exclaimed.

Reverend E. Life picked up a piece of paper, crumbled it, and tossed it to the side.

"Sometimes it is difficult to grab a problem and throw it to the side! How did this happen, Philadelphia?"

Reverend E. Life shrugged his shoulders and loosened his necktie.

"Tell it! Tell it!"

"Well, Philadelphia, some problems transcend time from generation to generation, legacy to legacy. Some problems, we bring on ourselves. We try to be something other than what we were made to be—a child of God!"

"Tell it! Tell it!"

"As children of God, we have to learn how to get along, Philadelphia! Children of God can't sing "Precious Lord, Take My Hand" when we are too mean to hold one another's hands!"

"Tell it! Tell it!"

"They don't hear me, Deacon Scott! How can we toss a problem to the side if we can't grab the problem? I will tell you how.

Philadelphia, when we pray, we should believe that we will receive!"

"Tell it! Tell it!"

Reverend E. Life unbuttoned his jacket.

"Mess rhymes with stress and with less of mess you will start to do your best! God will not forsake you! I feel you, Holy Ghost. Thank you for letting me feel your spirit!"

Deacon Scott stood from his seat.

"Tell it! Tell it!"

Behind him, the other deacons followed his lead. They clapped and cheered the preacher on. Reverend E. Life growled in his deep raspy voice as he picked up the black cordless microphone so that he could walk around the pulpit as he preached. The organ player played a melody that rose and fell with the preacher's voice.

"Hmm, there are people who think money will buy them love… hmm… but I am here to tell you, Philadelphia…mo money brings mo problems!"

Tomeka stirred in her seat. It was as if Reverend E. Life was speaking directly to her.

"If you want to know the true meaning of love, just read I Corinthians, chapter thirteen, verses four through eight. There it says, Love is patient and kind…hmm...love is not jealous or boastful...hmm…it is not arrogant or rude! Love does not insist… hmm…on its own way. It is not irritable or resentful, it does not rejoice at wrong but rejoices in the right…hmm…Love bears all things, believes all things, hopes all thing and endures all things!"

"Tell it! Tell it!"

"Hmm…Philadelphia…God so loved the world that he gave his only begotten son to bear all things and clean up any type of mess! Don't be tricked by what you hear on the radio or TV, God loves you,

Philadelphia, like he loved his only begotten son!"

Tomeka smiled as wide as she could. The decision she had to make was becoming clearer.

"Tell it! Tell it! Tell it! Tell it!" the congregation shouted.

"Philadelphia…hmm… the Lord will never lead you wrong! Psalms chapter thirty seven, verse twenty-three says…hmm…'the steps of a good man are ordered by the Lord'… He will never let you mess up"

"Yes!" Tomeka shouted.

Natalie looked at her daughter and nodded her head. She was glad that she was getting the message.

"Hmm…Isaiah chapter forty one, verse ten says, 'Fear thou not for I am with thee'…hmm…'be not dismayed for I am thy God'…hmm…'I will strengthen you and uphold you with my hand of righteousness.'"

"Yes! Lord," Tomeka continued to shout.

"So, what am I trying to say? Philadelphia, hmm, when the mess hits the fan, when adversity tries to get the upper hand on you and crush all life from you, hmm, know that your God will strengthen you and has not cast you away!"

"Tell it! Tell it! Tell it! Tell it!"

Reverend E. Life stepped from the pulpit. He knew it was time to save some souls. On the back row, Amere rocked from side to side.

"Today…hmm…on my way to Philadelphia…I felt that someone was going to need the Lord to move for them today and let them know that they were not going to mess up. My God, thank you for letting me feel your spirit. Today…hmm…I felt that someone had been betrayed by a friend who was supposed to be there till the end!"

Tomeka started to cry. Natalie patted her on the back.

"Yeah, there is someone here today…hmm…there is someone who has been tossed by the wayside when they have been to living on the high side in a high rise on the bayside! Jesus, thank you for letting me feel your spirit!"

"Tell it! Tell it! Tell it! Tell it!"

"Philadelphia…hmm…there is someone who is ready for a change to come into their life and move all of this nonsense and rigmarole out the front door! If you are here, say Amen!"

Tomeka and dozens of other worshippers shouted at the same time. The organ player's melodies escalated. Amere could no longer contain himself. He leapt to his feet and cheered the astounding preacher.

"Tell it! Tell it! Tell it! Tell it!"

"When you have a mess in your life…hmmm…Philadelphia, you need to have faith in the Cleanup Man…hmm…I got you now, Holy Spirit…Thank you for letting me feel your spirit…"

"Who is the Cleanup Man?" Tomeka asked.

"Well, He is the same one who was crucified on Friday and who rose with all power on Easter Sunday…hmmm…You know who I am talking about…hmmm…. He is first and then He is last …He is the beginning and the end!"

"Tell it!" Amere shouted.

"The Lord is A, and then he is Z…A, The Lord is access when mess blocks your way…B, The Lord is a bridge over messy waters… C, The Lord is a Cleanup Man when a mess needs to be mopped up…D, The Lord is a doctor who sits with his patients night and day!"

An usher started toward Tomeka as she began to shout.

"Yes, He is! Yes, He is!"

"E, The Lord is everything, yes he is...hmm...F, The Lord is
a friend that will not betray you in the end...hmm...G, The Lord
is good today....hmm...H, The Lord is my hope for a brighter
tomorrow...I, The Lord is my intelligence that never needs to be put
on trial...J, The Lord is a jealous God and will have no other gods
before him...yes, he is...hmm!"

"That's right! Tell it!" Amere shouted.

"K, The Lord is King of Kings....hmm...and L, The Lord is
Lord of Lords....hmm...M, The Lord is mighty, merciful, and makes
ways when there are no other ways...hmm... N, The Lord is all
you need...O, The Lord is an open door when all exits are closed...
hmm...P, The Lord will provide today and tomorrow just like he did
yesterday...hmm...Q, The Lord is the question but also the answer...
hmm!"

Reverend E. Life shook Deacon Scott's hand as they jumped
around in a circle.

"Tell it! Tell it," Deacon Scott yelled.

"R, The Lord is ready when others are still preparing...hmm...S,
The Lord soothes when I am in pain...hmm... T, The Lord talks
to me whenever I call upon him... My God...hmm...U, The Lord
understands my flaws and rights my wrongs...V, The Lord gives us
the victory before the battle is even fought...hmm...W, The Lord is
the wind beneath my wings...X, The Lord is an x-ray that looks past
that facial beauty and sees that ugly heart...hmm...Y, The Lord is
Yahweh the living God, and Z, The Lord is the zenith of everyone's
life!"

Reverend E. Life did a split in the middle of the floor and spun
around. The congregation's response was deafening.

"Tell it! Tell it!"

"Amen... Amen!"

"Thank you, Jesus! Thank you, Jesus!"

To calm himself just a bit, Reverend Life pulled a handkerchief from his pocket and dabbed at the perspiration that had formed on his brow. Then, he stretched out his arms in a welcoming gesture.

"The doors of the church are open."

Amere stirred in his seat as a sensational feeling engulfed him.

"If there is one who would like to join the body of Christ, please come forward and give your life to the Lord!"

Amere closed his eyes as the feeling expanded.

"This could be your last chance to get right, don't let it pass you by!"

"Here I come."

Amere stepped out into the aisle and walked toward his destiny.

17

Tomeka remained standing when Reverend E. Life extended the invitation. She did a triple take as Amere walked past her and sat down on the first pew where Reverend E. Life waited with outstretched hands.

"Mom, that is my friend!"

"What friend?" Natalie asked.

"The one I told you I met yesterday!"

Natalie had a confused look on her face.

"What? Who? Huh?"

"The guy who cooked me steak and shrimp last night! What is he doing here?"

"Why don't you go ask him? Maybe the Lord is trying to tell you something, Tomeka."

"You're right. He is. With Him, I can clean up this mess in my life."

Tomeka stepped into the aisle and went and sat beside Amere. She took his hand into her own. The feeling completed her. Reverend E. Life turned the microphone off and leaned forward.

"I can see the incorruptible bonds of true love bringing you two together."

"Yes, sir. I do love this woman."

"And I love this man," Tomeka said.

"My relationship counseling is every Thursday. Be there or be square!"

Reverend E. Life straightened up and turned the microphone back on. The church secretary took the names of the man and woman and presented them to the preacher.

"Two souls. Tomeka Washington and Amere Destiny. Young lady, I know who you are. You grew up in this church and you went away for a while. Your mother is Sister Natalie, am I correct?"

"Yes, sir. I have been away, but I want to rejoin the church."

"Well, it is good you have come back. Amere, I have never seen before, but there is something familiar about you."

Amere stood and addressed the congregation.

"My name is Amere Destiny. I have visited this church a couple of times, but, after hearing today's message, I want to join and serve however need fit."

"That will be arranged. We have a lot of work that needs to be done, especially with our young folk."

"Reverend, one more thing."

"Oh, I am sorry. This young man has a lot of words."

The congregation laughed as Reverend E. Life gave Amere the

microphone.

"Tomeka, I need some mess in my life to be cleaned up. Whatever mess is in your life, I will clean it up. Can we help each other cleanup with the help of the CLEANUP MAN from above?"

"Yes! Oh, yes!"

Tears of joy streamed down Tomeka's face as the congregation applauded! Reverend E. Life spoke into the microphone.

"I must be honest, church, for a man to be sincere about his deeds and intentions before the congregation speaks for itself. This man is blessed, and so is this woman.   The dates for your spiritual revival classes, as well as your baptism, will be announced at a later date. Right now, we want to welcome you into this church by giving you the right hand in fellowship."

Every one in the church started to sing.

"What a fellowship, what a joy divine, leaning on his everlasting arms…"

The deacons and mothers formed a circle with Tomeka and Amere in the middle. By custom, the members of the congregation each came around to shake their hands.

The process was short and simple. After the fellowship, Tomeka and Amere completed the basic information forms. After church was dismissed, Tomeka asked Amere the question that had been on her mind.

"So, you joined the church to see me and propose to me?"

"I confess, your honor. You got me."

"Be honest, Amere."

"Seriously, I wanted to hear the Word and see you at the same time. Is that a crime?"

"Not in my book. I want to introduce you to the most important people in my life."

They walked toward Natalie and Janicia. They had been waiting for Tomeka and Amere by the exit doors.

"This is my mother, Natalie Washington."

Amere reached out and shook Natalie's hand.

"I am very pleased to meet you, Mrs. Washington. You have a special daughter."

"Yeah, she is very special and touched but not by an angel!"

Amere burst out in laughter.

"I forgot to tell you that she was a comedian," Tomeka said. "Amere, I also want you to meet someone very special to me. The only thing that comes before her is God. Amere, please meet my daughter Janicia."

"Nice to meet you, Janicia."

Amere extended his right hand to shake hers, but Janicia ran behind Natalie's leg and said, "Nooo!"

"Janicia, don't be rude!"

This is it. This is what is going to cause Amere to run away! This is…

Tomeka's negative thoughts were stopped when Amere removed a pink set of car keys from his pocket and knelt down in front of the cute little girl.

"Janicia, my name is Amere Destiny. I know that you don't know me but I am a friend. As your friend, I bought you a car."

Janicia's brown eyes grew wide with surprise. Natalie nudged Tomeka in her side.

"I am too little to drive a car. I can't reach the pedal or see over the steering wheel," Janicia responded in her high-pitched voice.

"Well, this car was made just for you. It's outside. Come and look."

Amere opened the door and walked outside.

"That is my black Humvee over there, and your car is in the back of it."

"A small car for me? The big cars will run me off the road."

"You're right. That's why you can drive it on the sidewalk and in the parks. Let's go take a look at it."

Amere reached out, and Janicia took his hand. They walked down the stairs of the church then to his truck.

"I can't believe it. He has tamed the beast," Natalie said.

Tomeka and Natalie joined them at the SUV just as Amere popped the trunk. He reached in and pulled out a miniature black and pink Cadillac EXT utility vehicle.

"Janicia, you have soft seats, shiny wheels, and a radio," Amere said.

Janicia stepped into her truck and blew the horn.

"Momma, check out my whip! It's fly! Thank you Mr. Destiny! Thank you!"

"You're welcome. Now for you, Tomeka."

"You bought me something, too?"

"One second."

Amere opened the front passenger's door and took out a small box and a card. Tomeka opened the box and held up a silvery necklace with a diamond charm shaped like a capital 'T'.

"A diamond for my diamond."

"Thank you! Thank you, Amere!"

Amere put the necklace on Tomeka as she read the card.

"Just because…I woke up…Just because…the day began…Your

love has filled me up...Because of you, I am a better man...Just because..."

Tomeka turned around and looked Amere in his hazel eyes.

"I guess you are the cleanup man!"

"No, I am not the Cleanup Man, but I will be yours and Janicia's cleanup man if you will have me."

"I will!"

"I will, too!" yelled Janicia.

Amere stooped down and picked Janicia up as she tightly hugged him around his neck. Tomeka leaned forward and gave Amere a long passionate kiss.

Now, let's go get something to eat like every family does after church," Tomeka said.

"Mrs. Washington, I hope you hungry," Amere said as he turned to Natalie.

"Yes, I am but after this I may need to go find me a man! Let's go!"

Amere loaded Janicia's car into Tomeka's truck. As they followed him to a nearby restaurant, Amere realized that, for the first time since his injury, he felt complete. Tomeka followed Amere into a new beginning.

Another Title by G.S. Crews

Breinigsville, PA USA
10 September 2009
223867BV00001B/5/P